Caught in the Act!

"Duck!" A car rounded the courthouse square so Tuan and I pressed down behind the Pitt pig. It wasn't a squad car. Pittsfield has two. The lights moved past slowly, and since we were already crouched there, we tossed the toilet paper around the statue's little hog legs and wrapped its hams in blue.

All quiet again, we played high-flying pitch-and-catch, looping the rest around the branches. When that ran out, I grabbed the last roll, a green one. Carefully, I tore the paper loose, wound up, and tossed the stream of green toward the moon. "Identified Flying Object Streaks into Space," the headlines read. "Local Boy Sends Paper Path to Mars, Where Squat Red People Shriek Welcome!"

Suddenly we were in the spotlight. A real spotlight. It was bright and sharp and caught us like a net. The green roll fell, draping over the side of the pig and bumping down the courthouse lawn.

"What are you boys doing?"

HELLO, MY NAME IS SCRAMBLED EGGS

Jamie Gilson

Illustrated by
John Wallner

A MINSTREL™ BOOK

PUBLISHED BY
SIMON & SCHUSTER, INC.

"Yellow Submarine" (John Lennon & Paul McCartney) © 1966 Northern Songs Ltd. All rights in the U.S.A. and Mexico controlled by Maclean Music, Inc., c/o ATV Music Corp. Used by permission. All rights reserved.

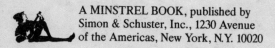

A MINSTREL BOOK, published by Simon & Schuster, Inc., 1230 Avenue of the Americas, New York, N.Y. 10020

Text copyright © 1985 by Jamie Gilson
Illustrations © 1985 by John C. Wallner
Cover artwork copyright © 1986 by James Warhola

Published by arrangement with William Morrow & Company, Inc.
Library of Congress Catalog Card Number: 84-10075

ISBN: 0-671-63578-6

First Minstrel Books printing July, 1986

First Minstrel Books special printing August, 1986

10 9 8 7 6 5 4 3 2 1

A MINSTREL BOOK and colophon are trademarks of Simon & Schuster, Inc.

Printed in the U.S.A.

TO SHARON STEINHOFF,

MY UNSCRAMBLER

CONTENTS

1 THE WHOLE THIRD FLOOR 11

2 SEE THAT KID? 22

3 THE STEPS MOVE 32

4 WHAT MEANS? 41

5 OK? OK. 61

6 FOLLOW THE DIRECTIONS 70

7 T.G.I.F. 86

8 AND THAT, YOU GUYS, IS THE NEWS 108

9 BOO! 120

10 THE SNOW DRAGON 135

11 PHO TAI AND PUMPKIN PIE 148

HELLO, MY NAME IS SCRAMBLED EGGS

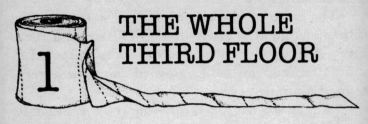

1 THE WHOLE THIRD FLOOR

STEAM CURLED UP from the brown-sugar mountains. I stirred my oatmeal, cut a slushy valley through the middle, and then whipped it around again fast. The whirlpool sucked at the galactic prisoners clinging to my spoon. They waved their tiny neon arms as they sank.

"Harvey," Mom said, sliding a Twinkie into my lunch bag, "you don't have to kill the cereal. I boiled it till it stopped screaming. Just eat it."

The wall phone rang and I grabbed it. "Harvey Trumble!"

Dad picked up the one in the bedroom. "Trumbles'! May I help you?" he asked, the way he does at the drugstore.

The voice on the other end was soft as cotton balls. "A good morning to you, Clifton. And Harvey. A very good morning to you both. This is Jeff."

"Morning," my father growled. He is not a very good-morning person.

"I'm calling to ask a favor," the voice went on. It was Jeff Zito, the minister of our church. I like listening to him. He plays his voice like an oboe—louds, softs, rests, and all.

My dad sighed. He doesn't much like Jeff Zito, who calls everybody, even the old people, by their first names, and asks everybody, even the kids, to call him Jeff.

"I'll do what I can," Dad said cautiously.

"Is it Pete, calling from California at *this* hour?" Mom asked. My brother, Pete, had been at college way over a month. He didn't call home much. I shook my head. She rinsed the oatmeal pan as she watched me listen. "Is it for you?"

I shrugged and hung up as Jeff began what he said was going to be a long story. Flooding my battle-strewn oatmeal with a wash of warm milk, I mooshed it around again and stopped thinking about Dad and the favor. That's nothing to me, I thought. What's to me is having a science quiz and a major math test, both on the same day. I wasn't ready for either. I'd spent the night before in the basement, zapping the sneaky Zagnabs Pete had programmed for our computer, Felix. I'd really leveled them, and Felix had said I was perfect. Felix is good company. We understand each other.

Six weeks into school, and it wasn't exactly a bag of gummy bears. Seventh grade was harder than sixth. For one thing, in every class you had a different teacher to get used to. Mr. Tandy, the guy who taught math, bugged me. He looked mostly up at the ceiling squares and thought everybody should understand what he was talking about the first time he said it. It might have been a Laff Riot if Eric Wagner had been there to laugh with me. Eric had been my best friend since I was two, but he'd moved to Pennsylvania over the summer, as far away from the middle of Illinois as Mars. Bummer.

"Hi, Harvey!" My sister, Julia, skipped into the room, wide awake and beaming. She *is* a good-morning person. She was dragging her stuffed owl, Zachary, behind her. Julia slept, thumb in mouth, with his wing clutched in her fist.

"You taking Zach to school today?" I asked. "He looks like your basic first grader."

"Maybe." She tossed her head. But she always left Zach at home on the boot box in the front hall. Zach was disgusting, more disgusting than a first grader even. He had fresh egg yolk on his belly from yesterday's breakfast. And that was on top of broccoli, brownie crumbs, and mottled junk from three years

13

of sandbox cities and finger paint. Plunking him onto a chair at the other end of our long kitchen table, she climbed up on him like he was a booster seat.

"Phoebe," Dad called from upstairs, "would you pick up the phone?"

"I don't want oatmeal," Julia said. "I want Froot Loops. So does Zachary."

Mom picked up the phone, but she didn't talk, except to say, "Hello."

"Today," Julia told me, "our class is going on a field trip." She climbed off Zachary and got the Froot Loops out of the cabinet. Then she took out five whole Loops and one broken one, carefully placing them on the oatmeal. "That's how old I am," she told Zachary, "almost six."

"Oh, how dreadful!" Mom said—to the phone, not to Julia. Actually, Julia's birthday is on Halloween, which *is* pretty dreadful. Not as bad as having one on Christmas, but, still, nobody wants to spoil a good Halloween appetite with birthday cake.

Julia poured just enough milk into the bowl to float her five-and-a-chunk circles.

"Where you guys going on your field trip?" I asked her. Not all that many places to go when you live in pint-sized Pittsfield, Illinois, known to its friends as "Pork Capital of the World." "You going to a pig farm and squeeze mud through your toes?"

"Oh, no," she said. "Better. We're going to our

14

teacher's house. I always thought she slept on the rug at school. She *could*. It's got two big pillows near the bookcase." Julia scooped the little O's out, one by one, and chewed them slowly. "Mrs. Broderick likes Big Bird. You think she'll have a Big Bird bedspread like mine?"

What a weird field trip, I thought. Going to see somebody's bedspread.

Mom was smiling at the phone, nodding her head as if we had Phone-a-Vision. I could imagine Jeff smiling back at his end, only he'd have had the receiver crooked in his neck so he could wave his arms. He's good at talking people into doing what he wants. Very good.

"Why, of course we will, Jeff," Mom said. "That way we'll get to know the folks well. Besides, it'll be an educational experience for Julia and Harvey."

Educational experience. That always means dull. And it usually means work. I just happen to know.

"Saturday's only two days away," she went on, "and it's short notice, of course, but that can't be helped. Harvey will be happy to . . ."

Julia began to eat fistfuls of cereal straight from the box, and the crunch was drowning out what Mom was saying I would be so happy to do. I clamped my hand over Julia's mouth and lifted the cereal box over her head. But, even covered, Julia's yells are louder than her crunches.

Mom frowned at us and walked the phone into the

15

dining room, trailing its long cord behind her. I gave the box back to Julia and dug into my oatmeal. But it was cold, and there's nothing more yucky than cold oatmeal. If there *had* been galactic prisoners in it, they'd have been begging me for down coats and moon boots.

Julia was still crunching away, hugging the box to her chest, when Mom turned the corner. Hanging up, she crossed her arms and smiled. "Well, here's a surprise for you."

And that's when she told us about the Nguyen family. I mean, we knew about them already, of course. That wasn't a surprise. Our church was sponsoring them. I hadn't paid that much attention, but I knew the family had escaped from Vietnam in a fishing boat. I knew they'd been living in a crowded camp in Malaysia, and that the church was bringing them to Pittsfield to start a new life. For weeks we'd been collecting clothes and furniture and stuff, and some men were putting a new furnace into a little house about half a mile from ours. They were our project.

"Butler and Freda Taylor were going to keep the Nguyens for the first two weeks," Mom told us, "to show them how to buy groceries and use the stove and such, but . . ."

Dad hurried in, tucking his shirt into his pants. "Phoebe, for crying out loud, you've got to learn how to say no."

"*You* could have said no," she told him.

"Can *I* say it?" I asked.

"No, no, no," Julia sang to the tune of "Three Blind Mice." She slipped off Zachary and grabbed his wing.

"Butler Taylor came down with chicken pox last night," Mom explained to Julia and me. "Imagine, a big bald man covered with all those spots. So, of course, the Taylors can't take the Nguyens. Their plane arrives in Chicago the day after tomorrow." She picked up a loose pink Froot Loop from the floor. "After all, we do have the whole third floor empty now, Cliff. It's all right. Pete's room is empty too. And we'll clean out the spare room. What shall we do with your beer can collection, Harvey?"

I've got this huge, mammoth beer can collection. My dad doesn't much like it, though, so it's been moved around a lot. Except for one really extremely valuable can, they were all packed in big black plastic trash bags that sat like blobs in the spare room.

"No, no, no," Julia chanted as she ran. "Harvey," she yelled from the front hall, "hurry up!"

"There's supposed to be a baby, *and* a boy about your age," Mom called to me as I ran. "Won't that be fun?"

Outside, Julia was puffing clouds of hazy breath, so I knew it was early fall cold. Grabbing my jacket, I dashed out to where she was running in place, waiting for me to walk her to school.

"What'll they be like?" Julia asked as we cruised. "The baby will cry all the time."

"Right," I said, "and wet. Babies do that." I tried to remember the things Jeff had told us about the Nguyens. He hadn't said what they'd look like. "Probably the kid my age will wear an embroidered green silk kimono and carry a sword in a black belt around his waist. And he'll yell, 'Aieeeeeeeee,' and crack concrete blocks with the side of his hand and have a fat black pigtail down his back." I grabbed one of her short brown ones and gave it a tug.

She flipped her head away. "Somebody in my Sunday school class brought jeans for the kid."

I shrugged. "He'll wear them under his kimono. He'll eat raw fish and rice and drink tea from a little cup."

"I don't like fish."

"Yes, you do. You eat tuna salad sandwiches all the time."

"That's not fish. It doesn't have eyes. I won't like the new kid—or the baby."

"I will. We'll be their heroes because we saved their lives."

"Hi, Zilch," a voice said close to my ear. It was Quint Calkins, sneaking up like a black cat at night. He spends a lot of his time being a pain, especially to me. Quint matched Julia's short first-grade steps. Then he reached over and pretended to take a quarter from behind her ear. Very big on magic, Quint

18

is. He whipped off his baseball cap and bowed. "If you washed back there, small child, you'd make a fortune."

Before Julia thought of demanding her ear money, four of her friends appeared from a side street, and they all ran off together, giggling like crazy about going to see Mrs. Broderick's bathroom.

"One of my two brand-new tricks," he said. "Worked pretty good, don't you think?"

I knew Quint was going to say something about math. On the first test of the year I'd gotten every problem wrong. A big fat zero, without even a smiley face in the middle of it. I just didn't understand the stuff. No kidding. Quint had gotten every problem right. Flashing silver stars. That's when he'd started calling me Zilch. I decided to bring it up myself so he couldn't.

"You study for the math test today?" I asked, laughing, ha-ha.

He didn't answer, just curled his lip in what was supposed to be a nasty grin. It was pretty good, actually. "So, I hear you're gonna have some company."

"Who said?"

"Jeff Zito said. He called my mom first because we've got that empty apartment over the garage, and my uncle being in that war in Vietnam and all. She told him thanks, but no thanks. Then she called back later to find out who'd said yes." Quint laughed like he knew something I didn't. But then, that's the way he always laughs. "Those guys moving in with you think funny, you know. That's what my uncle says."

We passed Julia's grade school and headed toward the junior high, three blocks on. No way I could shake him.

"Doesn't matter how funny you think they think," I told him. "The new kid is going to be staying at my house, and if you don't like him, you can just stay away. Anyway, before you know it, he'll be thinking just like me."

"And that's not funny?" He laughed like it was. "By the way, Zilch, the day won't come when I have to study for a math test. Mr. Tandy says I'm gifted. He told my mom that at Open House. Gifted. How's that sound? Gift-ed."

It sounded, actually, like he was saying it in calligraphy, every letter curly. I yawned. Big.

With his grubby paw, Quint reached into my mouth. I wish I'd crunched his fingers like bread sticks, but if I had, I'd have probably choked on Abraham Lincoln. Quint pulled a penny out from between my teeth, held it up, and bowed like I was a standing-room-only audience. Then he flicked it high toward the tree branches.

"Call it!"

"Heads," I said, automatically.

Just before it could reach the sidewalk, Quint scooped the coin up in his baseball cap, which he slapped tight over his black hair. I couldn't see which side landed up.

"Heads it is." He tapped the top of his cap and grinned. "*My* head. Can't say about the penny. Maybe, though, you've hit a winning streak, Zilch. Shall we take a look?" He glanced around to see if anybody was watching. A couple of kids had come up, and he motioned them closer.

As he whipped the cap off, a long green spring-snake flew out and zapped me, *splat,* in the nose.

"Tails!" he called. "Pity. You know, Zilch, you're gonna need some luck. You and your little clone, too."

2 SEE THAT KID?

CAROLINE QUACKENBUSH stopped me in the hall after school. "Harvey, are you going to T.G.I.F. tomorrow night, or not? I'm bringing double-fudge banana brownies." She and Suzanna Brooks were tacking up this poster they'd painted in ultra-violent pink and purple. T.G.I.F. PARTY! it yelled. 7 PM! DANCING! OPEN GYM! BASKETBALL! VOLLEYBALL! ‹FLOOR HOCKEY! BELLY LAUGHS! Something for practically everybody. The school has a T.G.I.F. every Friday night. I'd never gone.

"Not!" I had to shout. The hall lockers around us were clanging shut like tinny prison doors. "I've got stuff to do." I smiled Quint's I've-got-a-secret smile. "Maybe you didn't know. That Vietnamese family's staying at our house."

"You're kidding!" Caroline poked in the last thumbtack and twirled a loose strand of blondish hair around her finger.

"It's a long story. About . . . chicken pox." I changed my smile from secret to black-plague mystery.

"Really?" Suzanna moved in, aiming her fingertips at me. They were dotted chicken-pox pink with poster paint. She couldn't have twirled her hair if she'd wanted to. It's a tight Afro. "I expect you're scared. I know I would be."

"Oh, the Vietnamese guys aren't the ones who have chicken pox," I told her. "Jeff was afraid they'd catch it from Mr. Taylor, who's like one big red itchy spot."

"That's not what I meant." She turned the water fountain on her hands, and the paint ran in little pink rivers down the drain. "I mean all the stuff Jeff told us in the meeting. I mean the things he said we had to remember. I'd be scared I'd forget."

Actually, I'd been trying to think what he'd said about the Vietnamese, but the meeting had been a couple of weeks before, and as he'd talked there'd been these two squirrels racing back and forth across the telephone wire outside the window and I'd thought for sure one of them was going to drop, *splat,* on the parking lot, but it didn't—so I wasn't listening too close.

"Oh, *that* stuff." Besides the squirrel tightrope runners, I came up with "He said they're leaving a land of water buffaloes for a land of snowmobiles and it won't be easy."

She nodded, waiting. Then I remembered more, which just goes to prove you don't really have to listen. "Well, of course, they don't shake hands," I said, as if that was the first of a long list of one through a hundred and one that I could've told her if I'd felt like it. "But I don't go around grabbing people's hands. Besides, what's the big deal if I forget?"

"You don't want to get off on the wrong foot. You don't want them to think right away that you're bizarre." Suzanna flicked her fingers, splattering pinkish water at me and my books.

"And, you know . . ." Caroline grabbed me by the shoulders and stared into my eyes like they were tunnels. She had to stare down because I'm about three inches shorter than she is. "They also think you're strange if you point at them." She let go of one shoulder and touched the tip of my nose with her finger.

"They do?" I struggled. With my hands full of books, it was hard to pull free. Sort of.

"Blue," she said, holding tighter. "I thought for sure they were green. Do you wear contacts?"

I broke loose. "Cut it out!" Caroline's eyes are brown with little specks of yellow. I just happened to notice.

"Watch your step, Zilch," Quint called as he passed by with a gang of kids. "That's deep water." A couple of them whistled.

"Caroline!" Suzanna was annoyed. "Neither of you listened to Jeff. I was taking notes. She put her hands on her hips. "So, here's what you're supposed to do. Hel-lo, my-name-is-Su-zan-na-Brooks." She said it like a record playing at half-speed. "Wel-come-to-Pitts-field. I-know-you-will-learn-to-feel-at-home." She was smiling like I was a TV camera. "See, you talk slowly so they'll understand. OK, now, you try it. I'll be the refugee person."

"Why, hi, there," I yelled. "My name is Attila the Hun, and you get to stay at my house, you lucky kid, you. Just stick with me."

"Attila," she told me, "the 'stick with me' stuff was wrong. Jeff said you're not supposed to use slang like that or like 'I've got to hit the books.' But I think you're not big on book-hitting, anyway." She giggled. At least she didn't call me Zilch.

"I'm late for work." I backed up, but she was sticking with me like Velcro.

"Try not to *shout* because they're not deaf, they just don't speak the language. I wish I had my notes. They don't call people over by motioning with their index finger," she went on, "because that's the way

25

they call dogs." I could tell she'd said she was scared she'd forget just so she could tell me how much she remembered.

"If you need any help . . . " Caroline said.

I dashed out the front door, free. Actually, I did need help. On Thursdays, Fridays, and half-day Saturdays I worked at Mom and Dad's drugstore. We were starting a big twenty-percent-off sale on Friday, and so I had to finish out the afternoon zapping hundreds, maybe thousands of red New-Low-Price stickers onto toothpaste boxes, Odor Eaters, patterned panty hose, bunny-rabbit barrettes, and like that. Pete and I used to fool around a lot in the stockroom, pricing each other's noses and stuff as we worked. It was fun. When I was there by myself, though, the stockroom was a dungeon with prisoner me hemmed in by hissing drugstore serpents, rare and deadly.

I sprinted down the sidewalk toward the town square, parting a tide of yellow leaves, slowing down through the oatmeal-cookie smell that drifted out of Miles' Bakery, and stopping, finally, at the big metal "Pork-Capital-of-the-World" pig statue on the courthouse lawn. It's made out of old car parts welded together. Sort of modern. Pittsfield doesn't need George Washington on a horse. Pitt Pig has class. I pushed its fat spring snout. I always push it for luck, expecting a whole-hog genie to shoot back out, *shazam*. There has to be one in there somewhere, grunting wishes.

But this time I didn't need it. I already had my wish. I was getting a kid of my own to take Eric's and Pete's places, a kid I could teach whatever I wanted to. He was coming from rice paddies, and I was going to program him so he'd understand *People* magazine. There was this Vietnamese girl I'd either read about there or seen on TV who was in the finals of the Great American Spelling Bee. She'd been in this country no time at all, maybe less, when she'd won. Some kid had probably taught her *I* before *E* except after *C* and, so they say, in *weird neighbor,* and *weigh.* Then, of course, the teacher kid had clapped like crazy whenever she won a round. I could hear the wild applause as I opened the door to our drugstore.

"Harvey," Dad called from behind the prescription counter, "fill the Coke machine before you start pricing. Where've you been? Your mother marked all the deodorants this morning, so just start with the toothpaste. I've already unpacked it."

I chucked cans into the Coke machine.. Then I flattened the cardboard boxes Dad had emptied during the day and stuffed them into the garbage bin.

A big batch of lemon-flavored PURE toothpaste was stacked on the stockroom counter. I didn't know how we'd sell that much unless everybody in town really did squeeze it out snake-thick, like they do on TV. With a little curl on top. The PURE had been $2.49, so I figured out the big fat discount and set the pricing gun. The stuff tastes the way furniture polish smells. Yucky. So I covered the RE with a red sticker. PURE. *Zap*, $1.79. PU. After pricing a few, I made a square of boxes to build on and started adding layers up. *Zap*. And up. *Zap*, $1.79. PU. Winner and still champion in the price-gun category is . . .

"Harvey," Julia called. "Hi." Lowering her head, she ducked under the swinging door that leads from the drugstore into the stockroom. "Mom had to go to a meeting. She said you should baby-sit me. Dad said not to bother you, OK?"

I put $1.79 on her nose.

She emptied out the brown-paper sack of Hot Wheels she was carrying and sat down on the floor next to a carton of pH-Perfect Strawberry Shrub Shampoo for Oily Hair. "*Rnnnnnnnn, rnnnnnnn,*" she purred and raced two trucks up my leg.

"How was the field trip?" I asked her, zapping and stacking like a robot. "Learn anything you didn't know?"

She let the trucks crash on my shoes. "Mrs. Broderick's bedspread doesn't have Big Bird on it, or Kermit, either. It's got pink roses. Her bathroom has pink towels and pink toilet paper and pink soap. And she's got a dog named Maudie."

"Who is, naturally, pink." My stack was getting to

be Mt. Everest with only a half-carton of toothpaste left to go.

"She sings," Julia went on. "I mean, she barks 'Jingle Bells,' and you can *really* tell."

"Mrs. Broderick?" I asked.

Julia laughed. "No! *Maudie.*" She climbed onto a stool next to me and handed over a box of the revolting toothpaste. I zapped it.

"Mom's getting me a dog just like Maudie." Julia's Jeep popped a wheelie on the counter. "I'm going to teach it to bark 'Glory, Glory, Hallelujah.' "

"Who says?"

"Me." She narrowed her eyes at my toothpaste mountain.

"You knock that over, kid," I warned her, "and I'll wind you up and aim you at the moon. Look, our last dog chewed up Dad's sunglasses, dug out Mom's parrot tulips, and ate Pete's sneakers, so don't get your hopes up. Said dog now lives on a farm, where he bites strangers."

"My Maudie will be good."

"Don't hold your breath."

"Can you add one more box on top?"

"Maybe." I raised my arm high and carefully placed a toothpaste box upright, like a flag, on the summit. It looked terrific.

The pricing gun clicked empty, and so I filled it with a new roll of red stickers. Julia drove the Jeep around the base of PU mountain.

"Look, I thought Dad said you weren't supposed to bother me."

She grabbed the box I'd just marked and wandered out toward the store. "I wanted a candy bar, anyway."

Zap, $1.79. *Zap.* OK—so, like Suzanna says, I thought, I don't shake this new kid's hand or point at him. Big deal. But I kind of push ENTER and start feeding him Useful Information. Before long he'll dress like me, talk like me, and act like me. Caroline, and even Suzanna and Quint, will say, "See that Vietnamese kid over there? After one *month* he could count to a hundred and knew about *I* before *E.* He scores eighty thousand when he plays Donkey Kong, knows all the verses to 'America the Beautiful.' And everything, *everything* he knows he learned from Harvey Trumble." *Zap,* $1.79. I'll just shrug, I decided, and tell them, "It's nothing, folks. No kidding, it's nothing." *Zap,* $1.79.

"Finished," I yelled. "On to the panty hose."

"Harvey," Dad called from out front. "You know, don't you, that twenty percent of $2.49 is $1.99. Did you do many of those boxes wrong?"

Not many. Just all. I closed my eyes and took a deep breath. "Julia!" I called.

She swung through the door and gave me a bite of her frozen Snickers. Then she drove the Jeep from one side, and I aimed a Thunderbird from the other, and we crashed the whole mountain down to the counter, making heaps of yellow PU toothpaste foothills.

Julia started handing them to me one by one. We were an assembly line. Grab, $1.99. Grab, $1.99, faster and faster.

"And he beat his old record, folks," I could hear the TV anchor announce breathless. "After the toothpaste market collapsed, Harvey Trumble boldly raised the price and saved the world from unsightly decay." Grab, $1.99.

Well, I decided, that new kid's going to have to do *something* for himself. Maybe percents.

3 THE STEPS MOVE

FRIDAY AFTER SUPPER I scoured the john, scrubbed the mold out of the cracks in Pete's shower, and dragged my beer can collection down to the basement, hoping the good ones wouldn't rust. I didn't even have time to stick around down there with Felix A. Computer, who was probably glowing a chip from pure loneliness.

Five people were supposed to be moving in—Mr. and Mrs. Nguyen, the baby, the kid, and their grandmother. So Mom and I set up Pete's room for the parents, the little sewing room for the grandmother, and the spare room for the kids. As I worked, I began to make plans. I'd show the kid once around town—the school, the courthouse with its fancy old stained glass, the drugstore, the cream puffs at Miles', the park where the swimming pool is, and Suicide Hill where you can skateboard when you get good. Probably we wouldn't look at the roses on Mrs. Broderick's bedspread, though her singing dog was a possibility.

What's more, they were even letting me go to Chicago with Jeff to pick up my kid. Dad should have gone in place of the man who was all puffy with chicken pox, but even though he has extra help on Saturdays, he couldn't take this one off what with the sale and all.

It was kind of bizarre, actually, because Jeff and I finally tooled away in the church's blue van at three-fifteen in the morning. The plane was supposed to arrive at eight-ten, and it's roughly a four-hour drive when there aren't flat tires or wrong turns. Mom made me go to bed, of course, but I didn't have much time to sleep before the alarm went off.

As Jeff and I headed out, nobody was on the streets, and the traffic lights on the square were just set to flash caution. The drive up to Chicago is over flat Illinois farmland, dull in the day, and nothing much at night but truck headlights barreling past. I dozed. Off and on.

The sun was hardly up when Jeff shook me awake.

It was almost seven-thirty, and he was starting up a spiral of curves on the airport garage ramp. As he pulled into a place near the elevator, I rubbed my eyes and shook the sleep away so we could head off to the waiting room.

One of those moving-belt sidewalks that lets you stand still carried us a block or so underground. Then we got on an escalator up to this huge hall where people were waiting in line with their suitcases and backpacks. After Jeff stopped to ask directions, we headed off again to file through a little arch where they discovered we weren't carrying any dangerous weapons.

I still can't imagine where so many people were going so early in the morning. Jeff said several refugees were supposed to be coming in on the same flight, and so a translator was at the gate to help out. A woman from Travelers Aid was there, too. Other sponsors waited around in clusters, talking to each other about families they'd had before and how they were doing. It was like a party.

"Flight 231 from San Francisco now arriving at Gate H-12," a voice on the loudspeaker announced. The party broke up as the greeters pushed closer to the door. I unrolled a kind of banner the fourth-grade Sunday school class had made out of white shelf-lining paper. WELCOME TO PITTSFIELD NGUYEN FAMILY, it said. The edges were red, white, and blue stripes. All we needed was a brass band.

A lady in a wheelchair was first off. She didn't look Vietnamese. Then came a few families and some men and women wearing ties and carrying brief-cases. This really cute girl in pink jeans and a fuzzy jacket flung her arms around a sailor as soon as he stepped into the waiting room. Traffic stopped while she gave him this massive kiss. But pretty soon the first Vietnamese appeared behind them. Twenty or so followed after him, edging around the smoochers, who were very glad to see each other. Once they stopped kissing, they rubbed noses and giggled. I couldn't help but notice.

Forget handshakes, I thought. I bet those Viet-namese are wondering what they'll do when we rush up with hugs, kisses, and public nose rubs.

The woman from Travelers Aid and the translator stepped forward to greet the cluster of anxious-looking Vietnamese who were hugging shopping bags, packages tied with twine, and tote bags that said C.A.R.E. on them. When the people looked up, they saw us all standing there with signs and things, beaming. They smiled back.

This is going pretty good, I thought. I raised my arms high over my head and waved the sign. It still felt like a party. WELCOME TO PITTSFIELD NGUYEN FAMILY, I waved back and forth. Several of the group glanced at the banner and blinked a few times, but no one came running up, hands behind backs, to say, "That's us!" There were quite a few kids, but

I didn't see any groups that looked like ours. What, I thought, lowering my sign, what if they'd missed the plane?

The Vietnamese translator, though, hurried over. "Perhaps I can help you," he said quietly. "Your sign may not be enough. *Most* of the families just arriving are called Nguyen. Are you the only sponsors from . . . ?"

"Pittsfield. Yes!" Jeff filled him in with the details we had and showed him the papers he was carrying with him. "Are all of these people, then, from one big family?"

"Oh, no." He smiled. "It is just that more than half the people in Vietnam are named Nguyen. It's a name like Smith—only *more* common. If I visit Pittsfield, I know from your sign that I will be welcome. My name, too, is Nguyen." He bowed slightly.

We said, "How do you do," and watched him go off in search of our family.

That was actually the first time we'd heard it pronounced "N-gwyn." All of us—even Jeff and the committee—had only just seen it printed. We'd been saying "N-*guy*-en." Jeff and I were practicing the name out loud when the translator came up with three people, none of them wearing fancy samurai costumes. There were a short man and a small, thin boy with no long pigtail but black hair cut in bangs. He looked younger than me, shorter,

36

too—which is really something, since I'm the kid in class they call Shrimp. An old woman dressed in gray stood back a step from them. Her face was wrinkled with lines deeper than any I'd ever seen, even on old farm women. Her eyes were black and damp-shiny, so small they seemed like part of the furrows. She looked as though she had never smiled.

The translator said their names, but they sounded so strange to me, I couldn't have said them back. Suzanna would have been proud of me, though. I clenched my hands in my pockets. "Hi," I said, long and slow.

Jeff stood, legs apart, hands crossed behind his back, nodding his head like a handshake. The boy and his father smiled really big. They reached their arms toward us.

"Hello," they said together, hands out. I started to laugh. I couldn't help it. Jeff and I both shot our hands back at them so fast that when we finally shook, our arms crossed like an X. I kept laughing like I had hiccups. My kid and his dad were staring down at the floor as if they wished they were back in a combat zone, anywhere but there.

"Excuse me," Jeff said to the translator, and he explained what we'd learned about handshakes.

The translator nodded. "It's generally true what you say." He spoke to the man and my kid, and they grinned at each other, said something to the translator, and then they all looked at us and started to laugh. People around us were staring like I was wearing a KICK ME sign.

"Before your guests left the refugee camp in Galang," the translator explained, grinning, "they went to a meeting. Among the many things they learned was that Americans have customs new to some of them. They were told that when they met you they should shake your hands so you would like them."

So we shook hands again. And laughed. And even bowed a little. It was crazy.

The kid was still smiling. *"Harvey,"* I yelled, pointing at myself. *"Harvey Trumble,"* I repeated, trying to break the language barrier.

Then I remembered not to shout and that pointing is supposed to be gross. Or did somebody tell them we do *that* here too? Just in case they didn't, I lifted my hand to the top of my head to find someplace else to put it.

"Nguyen Tuan," he said, reaching out his hand. So that was the name of my kid. We shook hands again.

The translator stopped his explanations to Jeff to tell me, "You should call him Tuan. In Vietnam, we say our family name first. Here, of course, he'll be Tuan Nguyen."

"Tuan," I repeated, wondering how we were going to get along without this translator guy. Was

38

it because they lived on the other side of the world that they did things backward?

"It-is-pret-ty-cold-out." I-sound-ed-like-a-ro-bot. "You're going to freeze, no kidding." He was wearing blue shorts, a short-sleeved brown shirt, and blue rubber thongs like the ones kids wear at the beach in the summer. Not exactly forty-five-degrees clothes.

He smiled at me blankly. "Eeze no kidding?" he asked.

The translator was telling Jeff that Tuan's mother was sick and had to stay behind in the camp with his baby sister. They would come later. I didn't know what to say, and so I just grabbed a heavy green tote bag from the grandmother, smiled too big, and started backing up down the long hall. We had a long way to go to get to the lower level where the rest of their luggage was being unloaded from the plane.

As we walked, the kid kept glancing from side to side at the ads on the walls of, like, girls in bikinis riding bareback in Jamaica and giant chickens pecking at twenty-four flavors of popcorn. The hall narrowed as we skirted a tall wooden fence. The sign on it said, PARDON OUR DUST, A SHORT-TERM BOTHER, A LONG-TERM GAIN.

Shuffling around barriers, it took us a while to reach the down escalator. Jeff was the first one on. He held out his hand to Mrs. Nguyen, who was walking just behind him. She had reached the top of the steps when suddenly she stopped and gave a weak, small cry. Looking back at us, her eyes wide, she said something low and fast, and backing up, grabbed at her son. We all stared at Jeff, who was trying to run back up the steps that carried him steadily down to the floor below.

Tuan peered down the escalator and then tilted his head at me, blinking like he had just watched a cow cruise up to the moon. "Move," he said, amazed. "Steps *move.*"

I nodded. And though Jeff called and waved from below, and people kept stepping onto the stairs that moved down and down, the four of us at the top just watched. We didn't move with them.

4 WHAT MEANS?

"But why?" Julia asked. "Why wouldn't they?"

"Because, moppet, they're chicken," Quint explained. "My uncle says. You'll see." Quint was talking about the escalator story. I mean, it was too good *not* to tell. So I explained to all the kids in line at the potluck lunch how the three Nguyens had dug in their heels at the top and stared down. Two fourth-grade kids, Billy and Simon, thought it was the funniest thing they'd ever heard.

We'd driven to the church almost straight from the airport, stopping at home just long enough to go to the toilet and unload the bags and boxes. We arrived at the big bash around one-thirty. The committee had planned this special lunch so everybody could meet the folks right away. A WELCOME TO PITTSFIELD NGUYEN FAMILY banner like mine, only much bigger, was draped on a string across the big all-purpose room in the church. Under it, the food tables were packed with everything from celery sticks to sheets of coconut cake.

Tuan and his dad stood next to Jeff in a kind of reception line, like at a wedding, though their smiles weren't quite as beamish as when they had gotten off the plane. In a chair next to the wall, Mrs. Nguyen sat under a basketball hoop where red, white, and blue streamers fluttered every time someone opened the door. You couldn't tell what she was thinking, and you couldn't help but wonder.

"Why, Agnes Shorter, wonderful to have you with us this bright October day." Jeff's voice carried like he was giving a sermon. He reached for her hand with both of his. "Nam Nguyen, this is Agnes Shorter. Nam here is young Tuan's dad, Agnes. You heard about Tuan's mom being sick?" He reached over and gave Tuan's shoulder a squeeze.

The kid smiled and nodded. "Nam Nguyen," Jeff moved on to the next greeter, "this is Charlie Quackenbush, runs the grocery store. Nam was a soldier in the war, Charlie."

The two Nguyens stood there smiling, shaking

hands. A reporter from the *Pittsfield Examiner* flashed pictures.

"Don't look at the camera," she told them, and they looked.

"Hey, Tuan," I yelled, "aren't you hungry?" I motioned him over.

Quint laughed. "Here, pooch!" he said. "Naughty, naughty, Zilch. Nice boys don't use their hands like that." And I remembered that calling the kid by curling my finger at him was part of Suzanna's Forbidden List.

Jeff was talking to him, sending him over to us. I shrugged. "Anyway, I took them down the stairs, instead," I explained, wanting to finish up the story before the kid got there and thought I was making fun of him.

"So, what'd they think?" Quint made one of his crazy faces, crossing only one eye. "They think a big, bad dragon was going to suck them down its long steel tongue? My uncle says they believe in dragons." The kids laughed.

Tuan crossed the hall filled with people who'd taken off from Saturday chores just to see him. They watched him walk and called, "Hi, there," smiling. By the time he stood next to us, though, the kids were quiet. Not sure what to say or do, they stared down at their toes, and then over at Tuan's blue rubber thongs.

A couple of fourth-grade girls started giggling from the quiet, said quick how-are-you's and then hurried on down the food line.

"Let's eat," I told the kid. This, I decided, was the time to begin his lessons. I started scooping stuff onto my big white paper plate, naming everything as I dropped it from the spoon. I did it slow. "Raspberry Jell-O mold with marshmallows. Green-bean casserole with onion rings. Carrot sticks. Pickled beets. Fried chicken." I held up a drumstick so he could see. My plate was getting heavy.

"Flat-tires-and-gra-vy." Quint dipped up macaroni salad. "Mouse-traps-with-pic-kle-rel-ish." He was trying to ruin everything. Billy and Simon covered their mouths to keep from breaking up.

There was still some space left in the middle of my

plate. "Baked beans," I said louder to drown out Quint, "and," as I speared one, "a hot dog."

The kid gave me a funny look. "Hot dog?" he asked.

"Right," I told him, glad to hear him talk again. "I could eat them every day."

"You got to eat a hot dog," Quint told him. He stuck his fork into one and let it drop in the middle of Tuan's plate. "It's the all-American food."

Quint, Billy, and Simon followed the new kid and me to a long table with a huge pumpkin and some Indian corn as a centerpiece. We sat down and Tuan put his hands in his lap, watching as I squooshed the hot dog into the middle of a mound of baked beans. He picked up his fork and held it like he didn't know how. Showing it to us, he asked, "Name, please?"

"Name is *porcupine.*" Quint grinned. Billy and Simon poked at each other.

"It is *not.* Quint, stop being a jerk. It's called a fork. *Fork.*"

"Por-cu—?"

"*Fork.* Forget him. His name is Quint," I said, as though that explained it. Then I told him Billy's and Simon's names. They giggled like he was a TV show and couldn't hear them.

Everybody was eating as they talked. Wolfing it down. Saturday-noon starved. Except the kid. He was just watching. Carefully he shifted his fork to hold it the way we did, bent his head low over his plate, and kind of slurped some beans into his mouth with it.

"What'd you call a fork in Vietnam?" I asked. He didn't understand, and so I said it again slower, with motions.

He picked up his knife and fork and worked the two of them together with one hand.

"Chopsticks!" Simon yelled. And that's what it was. He was used to chopsticks.

"Here's how you do it, kid." Quint speared his hot dog in the middle, lifted it in front of him and began to bite from first one end and then the other. Billy and Simon loved it. They started doing the same thing, laughing so hard they couldn't swallow. Julia must have seen the hot-dog propellers from across the room because she came over and stood half behind me to watch, amazed.

"Eat hot dog many times?" Tuan asked Billy.

"Oh, sure!" Billy whirled away. "My mom says I should read on the label what's really *in* them, but she doesn't know what she's talking about. I eat them just about every day."

"I learn dog is . . . friend . . . here."

"Pet," I told him. "The word is *pet.*"

"Pet. Not pet in Vietnam. Dog eat too much." He watched Simon twirl and bite. "Please, you eat cat, too?"

"Eat cat!" Simon said. "Yuck."

"Double yuck." Billy put down his fork and moved away from the kid like he had something catching. "I think he thinks these things are made out of real dogs."

"Why not?" Quint pushed his plate away. "They make your stomach growl." Then he got up and gave a little bow. "Kid, I think you should know this. Here in the U.S.A., we eat our dogs hot. Cats we eat cold."

Julia's lip began to tremble. "Are hot dogs really made out of . . . ?" She couldn't finish. "Like Maudie? Is that why they're called . . . ?"

"Really, truly," Quint told her with a straight face. He bowed again and said, "Quint go. See you around, Hot Dog."

Billy and Simon grabbed their half-full plates, dumped them into the garbage can, and followed him. "Wait up!" Billy yelled.

Julia ran too. "Mother!" she called. "Is it *true*?"

The kid looked at the food on his plate like he thought it might suddenly start to sing and dance.

"It's not dog meat," I told him. "It's just pork." I cut a chunk off my hot dog and jabbed the air with it. "Pork!"

"Pork." He nodded.

Now he thinks it's called a pork, I decided, so I dug a pencil from my pocket and drew a curly-tailed pig on the paper tablecloth. "Pig," I said. Information In.

"Pig," he repeated cheerfully. "Yes."

It occurred to me that the Information In hadn't connected.

"Pig is pork." I bit my lip. It wasn't all that easy. "Hot dogs are pork."

The kid smiled. "Yes?"

Harvey, I thought. You've done it again. It's your two-plus-two-equals-two-hundred-twenty-two act. Then the old light bulb flashed on over my head. I put an equals sign after the pig and drew a hot dog.

"Oh, yes?" he said. "Hot pig." He speared it the way Quint had and bit off the end. "Good."

"Does your father speak English?" I asked.

"Father . . . " He glanced over to where his father

and grandmother were now eating with a big group. "Father is speaking . . . a little."

"How come *you* know so much?"

"I"—he shrugged—"no . . . no good."

"But who *taught* you?" Somebody had gotten to him before I could.

"American man. Mr. Larkin. At Galang camp." He reversed the hot dog and took another bite. "We wait in camp many month. First we come from Vietnam in boat. Then in Galang we wait. Mr. Larkin look for sponsor for us in America. Mr. Larkin say, 'Tuan learn English. In America must have English.' He say, 'Tuan help family. Tuan learn English.'" He flipped the hot dog and bit again. It looked like fun. I speared mine in the middle and bit it. "I try. I be American quick."

"Sure. I'll teach you English. I spoke it since I was a baby. It's easy."

He shook his head. "Very hard. Some sounds hard. Also, in Vietnam no say, 'Today I *eat*. Yesterday I . . .'"

"Ate," I finished for him. He was repeating a lesson. I could tell. "Yesterday I *ate*. Tomorrow I *will eat*."

"Will eat. Vietnamese say, 'Today I eat. Tomorrow I eat. Yesterday I eat."

"No kidding? That sounds easy."

"Yes?" Then he leaned forward, really interested.

49

"What means *no kidding*? You say many times, 'No kidding.' "

He had me. What does *no kidding* mean? I didn't want to seem dumb. I say it all the time. I had to know what it *meant*. I cleared my throat. "Well, sometimes," I explained, "it kind of means, like, 'Wow!' "

"Wow," he repeated, and waited.

"Sometimes it means, like, 'Do you *really* mean that?' "

He smiled at me mildly and said, "Yes?"

I was getting nowhere . . . again. "Sometimes it means 'That's true,' like when I say, 'I've got seven hundred fifty beer cans in my collection, no kidding.' " Well, maybe I didn't have quite that many, but I figured he didn't know numbers anyway, and seven hundred fifty is such a good round number.

"No kidding," he said.

"You got it!" I yelled, but he didn't, of course. He was just repeating.

"You guys thirsty?" Caroline smiled from across the table. She held out two big ice-filled foam cups. Suzanna was with her, hugging a big pitcher of tea. They'd just come from twelve-thirty band practice at the high school down the street. So had a lot of other kids who were probably eating second lunches, scooping mashed potatoes and hot pigs onto their plates.

Caroline sat the cups in front of us while Suzanna

put the pitcher down, crossed her hands behind her back, and looked at Tuan like she was memorizing him. "My-name-is-Su-zan-na-Brooks," she said.

The kid reached his hand toward her as if he'd done it all his life. "Hi," he said.

Suzanna stepped back. "Why is he doing that?" she asked me.

"He shakes hands." I looked at Caroline, and she winked at me. The hairs on the back of my neck tickled. Suzanna wiped her palm dry on her skirt, and shook his hand.

"Yes, thank you." I raised my cup to her. Frowning, she grabbed the pitcher and filled the cup with tea, clinking the ice. Then she poured some into the kid's cup, sneaking a look at him out of the corners of her eyes.

I reached for the bowl of sugar next to the Indian corn and heaped in three spoonfuls.

"Want some sugar?" I asked him. He smiled but didn't seem to understand. Maybe the computer in his head didn't have *sugar* yet. Harvey Trumble to the rescue! *"Sugar."* The crystals cascaded into his cup like a snow slide. He repeated the word, and I glanced at Suzanna to see if she was impressed.

"Your mother told me to tell you to meet her in the parking lot in five minutes," she said.

"His name is Tuan." I pushed the cup toward him. Tea is a big thing in Vietnam and places like that. Everybody knows it.

51

"You like it here yet?" Caroline asked him, taking it slow.

"Yes," he told her, waited a second, and then added, "no kidding."

Suzanna gagged. "No *kidding*?" She looked at me with her mouth hanging open. Nothing she could say. This was going much better than I could have hoped. Quint thought he was being funny, but the kid was almost a Harvey clone already.

Stirring the sugar that had sunk to the bottom of my cup, I picked it up and chugged it down. The tea was sweet, cold, and terrific.

The kid watched and then raised his foam cup and started to chug the way I had, but somehow it didn't work for him. His eyes opened wide. He choked. He gasped and, trying to catch his breath, flipped the cup upside down on his plate. I tried to remember the Heimlich maneuver.

His plate was awash, the paper tablecloth was spreading brown, and his blue pants were soaked from the overflow. Suzanna banged him on the back.

"I bet he likes it better hot," Caroline said. "*Better hot?*"

When the kid caught his breath he said, "Snow."

"Ice," I corrected him. "Ice."

Either that or he was telling Caroline no. Anyway, after we had soaked up a batch of paper napkins on the table and on Tuan, Suzanna and Caroline grabbed their jackets and clarinets and we all trekked out into the big gravel parking lot in back. My mom, Julia, and the rest of the Nguyens sat patiently in the station wagon. Billy, Simon, and Quint were skidding their bikes in the stones.

"Well, well," Quint called, "if it isn't the Hot Dog himself"—he pulled up in front of Suzanna—"with a genuine dill pickle." She scowled. "And that hilarious kid Harvey must have said something really wacko to make the Hot Dog laugh that hard." He pointed to Tuan's pants. Billy and Simon nearly wet theirs laughing.

"Ignore him," Suzanna told Tuan.

"That's OK." Quint shrugged. "He doesn't understand a word I'm saying."

"That doesn't make it right to say, you dolt." Suzanna gave his bike a push.

The kid shivered. "You didn't bring a coat, did you?" I asked him. I couldn't remember whether Mom had given him one to wear. "Do-you-have-ever-y-thing?"

He stopped suddenly, reached into his wet pants pocket, and, smiling, pulled out a small green fabric bag. He sighed, like he was glad to find it still there. It was drawn tight with a string, and soaked with tea.

Quint wheeled in to look. "What's he got?"

"Quint!" Suzanna shook her head. "You'd be a great kid if you'd start minding your own business."

He shrugged. "Just being friendly."

But the kid seemed to *want* to show us. And even Suzanna stared at the bag as he squeezed it dry, untied the string, and stuck his fingers inside. First he took out a couple of small metal balls that looked like ball bearings, wiped them on his shirt, and put them in his dry pocket. Then he picked out what I thought might be a jewel, an old family treasure, maybe, he'd smuggled in to sell for a million dollars. But it wasn't. It was a marble, about an inch across, clear, with a bright blue eye-shaped wedge set deep in the middle.

He held it to the light so we could see and then placed it on his palm. The marble shone as if it might have been a tiny crystal ball full of fortunes about mysterious strangers and long ocean trips.

"Name, please?" the kid asked.

"Marble," I said quick before Quint could tell him it was a toenail. "Marble."

I was about to ask if the bag had more in it like the blue one when we heard "Aieeeeeee," on both sides of us. Then "Aieeeeeeeee," the yell came again, and louder. Billy and Simon, screeching, were heading straight at us on their bikes like they meant to weave us between their spokes.

We scrambled. They hit the brakes and swerved, turning completely around and raising a spray of gravel. Caroline and Tuan both panicked, ran head-on, and slid across the stones in opposite directions.

Billy hopped off his bike. "Hey, we're sorry. We thought you'd trust us."

"We're good," Simon explained, wheeling up. "We do it all the time. It kills tires, though. Are you maimed?"

"What a stupid. . . ." Caroline's barrette had sprung free, and she blew the hair out of her eyes.

The kid got to his feet fast. You could see pink gravel dents in his elbows. The minute he was up, though, a scared look flashed across his face, and he dropped back to his knees, saying something I couldn't understand. He shuffled through the stones in a circle around him and then held up an empty cupped hand. The marble was gone.

Quint started searching on hands and knees. So did Suzanna. Caroline, winded, sat with her clarinet case in her lap.

"What are we looking for?" Simon asked.

"The Hot Dog's marble." Quint sat down on the stones and leaned against Caroline while the rest of us crawled all over the lot. Mom even came and searched. But there was no telling where his marble had flipped. Those guys had tornadoed the gravel.

"You'll just have to try tomorrow," Mom said finally, with a sigh. "We have to get these folks home. They're tired."

And so we were all gearing up to go, discouraged,

when Quint suddenly sprang to his feet like just-popped toast.

"You're not going to believe this, Hot Dog," he said, clamping his hand on Tuan's shoulder, "but I know where that marble is." We all stared at him. I mean, he'd watched us hunt for maybe ten minutes without saying anything. "I personally wouldn't have believed it if I hadn't seen it with my own eyes, but . . . " He made a big thing out of reaching into my jacket pocket. Whipping out his hand, he held the marble up between two fingers. "Harvey, your new buddy Harvey, had it all the time." Handing the marble to Tuan, he slapped me too hard on the back.

The kids all rolled their eyes and groaned. They knew Quint and his magic tricks. He was famous for them. Suzanna chased after him till he hopped onto his bike and outraced her to the street.

But Tuan didn't know Quint. For all he knew, he *was* staying with Attila the Hun—pillage, plunder, and all that. I shrugged my shoulders, threw up my hands like, "What're you going to do?" and added a weak "ha-ha." I mean, how do you say "sleight-of-hand" to a new kid using first-day words?

So I laughed. Tuan, too. Probably he thought he had to. And then we all headed for home.

As soon as we got there, Mom hurried the adults up to their rooms and told me to settle Tuan in his.

It was just four o'clock, but the Nguyens were really jet-lagged.

The kid and I stopped on the second floor. "You can use my shower," I told him, grinning about two sizes too big. I wanted him to be sure I really *was* a good guy. "See, there's only one bathroom upstairs where you sleep, and it'll be pretty busy with both your dad and grandmother." I was flinging out too many words. He didn't show a flicker of understanding.

"Shower," I said, and did a wild charade of it, jumping around and scrubbing under my arms like a monkey. Then I took him into the bathroom off the hall, turned the water on to a good warm, and gave him a brand-new bar of soap. I folded a pair of my last year's Cubs' pajamas on the edge of the sink and pointed to them. "For you."

Outside, I waited to hear the shower door close to make sure he'd understood. It clicked shut, but I didn't hear singing. He'd stood in the shower, though, because when he opened the door to the hall, his head was soaked and water was dripping off the tips of his bangs. My pajamas were too big for him. The red neckband drooped, soaking up the rivers running out of his hair.

"Rub it dry." As I handed him a fresh towel, it occurred to me that I could do better than that. So I led him back into the bathroom, slid open the cabinet, and got out my little red hair dryer. Actually, Pete had left it behind, so it was mine by accident. I plugged it in and handed it to the kid. He didn't take it. Probably, I thought, he's not used to a hair dryer like this. Maybe he's not used to a hair dryer at all. So I grabbed it by the handle and pointed the tube-shaped blower at my head.

"Like that," I said. "See?"

I lowered it and showed him the switches, flipping the HEAT to the light orange circle for LOW and the AIR switch to where it says HIGH. The dryer hummed and vibrated warm. Information In? I smiled, user-friendly.

This time Tuan took the dryer when I offered it, letting it rest lightly in his palm the way he'd held the marble before it disappeared. Giving me a weird look I didn't understand, he raised the dryer to see it better. But the sudden high blast on his wet hair splattered water in his eyes and onto the bathroom mirror.

He took a quick, deep breath, pressed himself flat against the tile wall and stared down at the humming dryer. "Gun?" he asked me, aiming it at the floor. "Bang-bang?"

It *did* look like a gun. It really did. Handle, barrel, and all. It looked like a red space-age shooter that plugs in and has its triggers on the side. A fancy American laser, maybe. I'd never thought of it as looking like anything but a hair dryer before. Grabbing the cord, I yanked the plug out of the wall. The humming wound down. The kid looked at me like he didn't understand anything at all.

OK, I thought, so a few things had gotten messed up. I was going to have to press the CLEAR button and start over. Maybe we could just forget day one. After I'd turned his name around, I'd headed him down a metal dragon's tongue, called him like he was a mongrel pup, fed him dog-meat sausages, handed him a spear to eat with instead of two sticks, choked him with a gob of ice, stolen his blue-eye marble, and, to top it off, tried to get him to spray his head with laser beams, bang-bang. There must be an easier way to turn American.

Julia stepped in front of the open bathroom door. The kid had the dryer still in his hand. I was holding the cord. Over her head she was waving the sign I had carried at the airport. WELCOME TO PITTSFIELD NGUYEN FAMILY. She had it upside down.

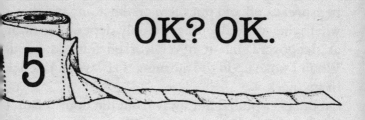

OK? OK.

5

"HARVEY, COME LOOK!" Julia called from the top of the third-floor steps. "They sleep funny."

"Quiet," I whispered and leaped the stairs two at a time to shush her. "Quiet, or they won't sleep at all." Still, it was the middle of Sunday afternoon, and they'd been up there almost twenty-four hours. The trip must really have zonked them out.

"Look at *that*," she whispered back and pointed into Pete's room.

The door was open and I could see inside. It wasn't true they slept funny. They were sleeping like people do, all curled up. It was *where* they were sleeping that was funny. They were all in Pete's bedroom, but they weren't in bed. They'd taken the bedspreads off and put them on the floor, and that's where they were sleeping. I'd only slept on the floor at sleepovers, but it never worked out too good. When I woke up in the morning, I always had a crick in my neck.

"Julia!" I pulled her away from the door. "Don't be nosy." And I headed her back down the steps. On the way, though, I coughed a little, hoping to wake the kid up. We had work to do.

When Tuan came downstairs about an hour later, he was a lot hungrier for food than for facts. He ate two apples from the bushel in the kitchen, some of the big bowl of rice Mom had made special, and a whole lot of beef stew. I would never have thought that using a fork could be so hard. Just watching him made me nervous. And I wondered how anybody could possibly eat all those slippery little grains of rice with sticks.

Right after he ate, I steered him down to the basement to meet Felix, trusty computer. I figured that since I'd pretty much blown the first day, Felix and I could program him with some basic stuff on the second. We sat on the tall red stools in front of the workbench Dad had built, and I slipped in the Dancing Demon disc to get the kid used to the keyboard. You don't have to do much. The demon on the screen just dances fast or slow, doing whatever steps

62

you tell him to. Then I shot at a few of Pete's personal Zagnabs and, after that, we both played this great game where you've got an aerial view of a fat robot that blips in with an ax and a shield in one corner and a skinny robot with an ax and a shield in the other and they go at each other. Tuan was the fat and I was the skinny. I creamed him. He'd seen TV, he said, so the computer didn't really knock him out. I mean, it wasn't like the escalator or the hair dryer. He didn't think I was trying to execute him with my joystick.

I'd decided it was time for Felix to teach him some new words. The first one would be *marble*. My dad had dug out a wrinkled leather pouch of his old marbles and given them to me so I'd have something in common with the kid. I mean, it wasn't as though I could shoot marbles or anything like that. My dad said it was an old American sport, but since I wasn't an old American, I didn't play it. Anyway, I opened the bag and dug out a big yellow one with tiny bubbles in it and gave it to the kid, feeling as guilty as if I really *had* tried to steal his blue cat's eye. He looked it over but didn't remember what it was called.

"Marble," I said, and typed it out on Felix. "What is it called in Vietnamese?"

He typed DANH-BI. "Need mark through *d* and over *n*," he told me, but the computer couldn't handle that. "Say, '*đáñh-bi.*' "

It was hard to say. It didn't fit my mouth, and so I only tried once. He started to hand the marble back. "Keep it," I said, holding my hands behind my back. "Keep it." He put it on the workbench.

Pete's bike was leaning up against the wall, in storage till he came home.

BICYCLE, I typed out on Felix and, giving the handlebars a pat, said it out loud.

So did the kid. "Bi-cyc-le."

"Close," I told him.

XE-DAP, he typed. "And mark through . . ." He pointed at the *d*. "*Bicycle* is *xe-đap*."

"Shut up?" I asked. That's sure what it sounded like.

"Close," he said.

"Do you know what *shut up* means?"

"*Shut up*? No. What means *shut up*?"

"It means 'be quiet.' " I put my finger in front of my lips and said, "Shhhhhhhhhh." He nodded. "Shut up!" I yelled.

"You talk loud to ask be quiet?"

"Right. *Shut up!* That's the way to say it," I shouted.

"*Shut up!*" he yelled back, laughing.

"You boys all right down there?" Mom called down the steps.

"Fine," I told her. "We're OK."

"What means *OK*?" he asked.

"*OK* means 'good,' 'terrific.' Didn't that guy in

64

camp teach you anything? *OK* is basic. *OK* is the best. We'll have Felix tell you 'OK' every time you get a word right, OK?"

"OK."

We sat there for a long time with me teaching him words like *follow*. First I marched around behind him. "I *follow* you." Then I got in front of him and made him say, "I *follow* you." I was the leader. He was my follower. We did verbs like *throw* and *hide* and *laugh* and *vomit*. After we'd both acted them out, I'd write them into the computer. And Tuan would write in the Vietnamese word so he'd remember what the English one meant. Input, output. Input, output. It was terrific. We were working on *hiccup* when Mom called down the steps again.

"Harvey, you've got company. It's almost ten o'-clock, though, just about time for bed."

"Tuan just barely got up," I told her, "and he's got lots of work to do. Who's there?"

"Quint the Quintessential," he called down grandly.

Big deal, I thought. "Enter," I said, though, since nothing was likely to stop him. He took the steps slow and heavy, waving and grinning like the Jolly Green Giant. I turned back to the computer.

"Hi, there, Zilch," he said. "Having a good time with your new toy?"

"The computer's not all that new," I told him, punching a few keys casually.

"I wasn't talking about the computer." He grinned, and leaning with his mouth close to my ear, he whispered, "Uncovering the mysteries of the Orient?"

"No!" I pushed him away with my shoulder. "I'm teaching Tuan English."

He gave the kid a big hello like he was his biggest admirer and then circled around behind him and rolled his eyes at me. "So, why bother?" he asked.

"He's got to learn it. He starts school Friday, the end of this week. With us."

"You're kidding. Our *class*?"

"Why not? He's twelve. Mom says it's fixed so he can be with me."

Quint laughed through his nose. "He doesn't know his elbow from an escalator and he's going to be in the same class with *me*? Gifted old me? He ought to be in Julia's room."

Tuan was working on the words we'd programmed. OK, Felix printed, turning on his computer charm. OK, TUAN. The kid glanced at Quint, who clapped his hands, yelled, "OK!" and nodded as if the kid had just won the Nobel Peace Prize.

Tuan turned back to the computer, smiling. Quint rolled his eyes again.

"That foreign guy upstairs," he said, "I suppose he's going to our school too?"

"That's Tuan's father, and he's going to work," I

told him. "He's thirty-some years old, too old even for high school. Jeff Zito's going to teach him English. I looked over at the kid, but he was concentrating on the word *laugh* which I guess isn't all that easy to sound out. "Tuan's dad has a job as custodian at the Starlight Motel."

"You *are* kidding. Is that fixed too? My uncle looked for work at the Starlight, and they said they didn't have anything. You mean they lied to Wayne so they could give a job to some foreign guy? Boy, I'm gonna tell him, and he'll explode."

"Come on, Quint. We brought them here to help. That's the whole idea."

"My uncle was in that war in Vietnam, too, you know."

"Listen, Quint, it's getting late."

"Right. I came to talk to the Hot Dog."

"Why?"

Quint ignored me.

"Listen," I said, "his name is *Tuan.*" I didn't want him calling my kid Hot Dog.

"You *are* good," he said to Tuan, as Felix went OK once again.

The kid beamed back.

"Will you teach me marbles?" Quint asked him.

"Teach?" He turned away from the computer. "*Teach* you?"

"Right." Quint picked up my yellow marble from the counter. "Will you teach me how?"

"Yes." Tuan grinned at him. "OK."

"Tomorrow?" Quint was trying to take my kid away from me. That's what he was trying to do. He handed Tuan the marble *I'd* given him just ten minutes before. "My uncle wants to ask the kid some questions," he whispered to me, like we were both in on some big joke. "Wayne knows a lot of words in Vietnamese. He wants to look him over."

"Sorry. Tuan's busy with important stuff tomorrow and Tuesday and Wednesday and Thursday, and he starts school Friday."

"After school Friday it is, then. You come to my house Friday," Quint told the kid. "OK?"

"I've got to work after school Friday," I told him.

"I didn't ask you," Quint explained like I was a little kid who'd begged to tag along to a party. "OK?" he said to Tuan again.

"OK! Marbles." You'd have thought the president had invited him to breakfast at the White House, he was so pleased.

"See you around." Quint took the stairs two at a time, slamming the basement door so we'd have something to remember him by.

When the place had stopped shaking, I said to the kid, patiently and slowly, "You don't want to go to Quint's."

"Yes," he said, smiling broadly, "I go to him house."

"His house."

"His house. He is . . . Quint?"

"Yes, he's Quint, all right."

"Quint is OK. Right way to use OK?"

"Right," I said. But I sure didn't mean it.

6 FOLLOW THE DIRECTIONS

"HELLO, MY NAME IS JELLY," Julia said, staring at the name tag stuck to a jar on the kitchen table. She'd guessed wrong. It said, HELLO, MY NAME IS JAM. Tossing Zachary onto her chair, Julia climbed on top of him, leaned back, and stared up.

"Hello, my name is Ceiling. Is that right?" I nodded. "I can read *ceiling*! Maybe they'll let me skip first grade." She craned her neck to look at the sign again. "Are you sure that says *ceiling*? Mrs. Broderick says the snake sound, Sssssssssssssssss, is S. Silly Sally Ceiling. See, it's got to be wrong."

"Ceiling," Tuan said automatically, copying it

into a small notebook I'd given him. NEW WORDS, I'd printed on the cover. He was eating breakfast and hadn't noticed that one yet.

"Remember '*I* before *E* except after *C*,' " I told him as he wrote. He blinked at me.

I'd got the name tags from this huge stack left over from a party of Mom's where nobody wore them. The tags had little red wavy borders with HELLO, MY NAME IS printed on the front and sticky stuff on the back. I'd written about a hundred names of things on them in wide black Magic Marker. Then I'd matched them up, sticking them on the sugar bowl, the doors, floors, apples, toilet, computer, boot box. Every day after I came home from school, I'd take the kid around naming things for him. The house was beginning to look like a first-grade workbook.

"Hello, my name is Butter Dish," Julia said. "Harvey, make one for Zachary. He's jealous."

"That tag better not leave a mark on the ceiling," Dad told me, wiping his mouth with his napkin. "And the day you lay one on my scrambled eggs, you've had it."

Actually, I *had* made a Scrambled Eggs label, but I'd decided it would slide off, and so I'd just stuck it in my back pocket.

"Your father is absolutely right," Mom said. "If there's anything that flusters me, it's eggs that try to get too friendly. More toast, Tuan?"

He shook his head and leaned over his scrambled eggs with a fork, watching me closely as I ate. He waited a long time before picking up the bacon with his fingers as I did, making sure that's how Dad ate his, too. His grandmother sat by herself at the end of the table. He called her Ba Noi, which means, he said, "your father's mother." A white wool shawl Mom had found for her was tucked tightly around her like a cocoon. She was not having scrambled eggs for breakfast, but broth with noodles in it, first drinking the broth and then eating the noodles with chopsticks she'd brought with her.

"Get Tuan to school on time, now," Dad called, barreling out the back door. Then Ba Noi spoke. It was the first time I'd heard her talk since the escalator. She said something to Tuan—low, fast, and kind of sharp. Tuan answered her quietly, glancing around at us and then down at his feet.

"Is something wrong?" Mom asked him. "May we help?"

The kid shook his head and took a deep breath. I wondered if he was trying to think what to say or how to say it. "Ba Noi say I not . . . look good for school," he whispered.

He looked good to me. I'd told him what to wear —faded jeans, a striped T-shirt, and the red, white, and blue tennis shoes Mom had bought him the day before. Perfect.

"Tell her I say it's *very* American."

"She want me *very* Vietnamese . . . blue pants. . . ." He sliced across his leg with his hand to show he meant the short ones he'd worn when he arrived.

I laughed. "You dress like that and everybody'll think you're weird. Besides, in this weather you'd die of terminal goose bumps." I knew he hadn't understood that. "Cold," I said, shaking myself with a shiver. "Short pants are for summer."

"Hello, my name is Clock," Julia announced. "We're going to be late."

Tuan spoke again to his grandmother. She still did not look pleased. But we waved good-bye to her and to Mom and hurried off. Tuan was smiling as if he liked looking very American.

On the way, we worked on tree names and street names. I named. He repeated. Once we got to school, I showed him the water fountain, the john, and the trophy case. People kept saying, "Hi," and so I taught him a few of the kids' names, too. It was an educational experience.

Finally, I got him to the principal's office. Mr. Saine was on the phone when I poked my head in. ". . . will deal with that matter immediately," he told the phone, motioning us to come on in.

Mr. Saine stood up, way up. I mean, he must be six-five. Tuan came about to his belt.

"Hi," Tuan said, holding out his hand when Mr. Saine came over to greet us.

"Why, hello, young man." Mr. Saine shook his

hand, looking pleased by good manners and all that. "I've been expecting you. How's his English?" he asked me, his voice lowered.

"I'm teaching him," I said.

"Good, fine." He sat back in his chair and started looking through some papers. "First you take him to homeroom. And after that we'll line up some diagnostic tests to see where square one should be, since there aren't any transcripts. Understood?"

I nodded. The kid smiled, understanding nothing. I could read the look by now. Mr. Saine shuffled through a stack of papers on his desk. "Reverend Zito tells me your name is . . ." He clamped his hands together, took a deep breath, and pronounced it all wrong.

And that was when I got the idea. If the kid really did want to be an American and to be one fast, the name Tuan Nguyen wouldn't do. It wouldn't do any more than short pants on a cold day. You put that name in lights or across a headline and people would get it wrong almost every time.

"He's just decided to change it. The name you've got isn't right. It *used* to be Tuan Nguyen. But now he's going to be . . ." I tossed the sounds around in my head a few times until his name turned, without any problem at all, into . . . "Tom. His first name is Tom." Mr. Saine glanced at Tuan/Tom, who smiled and nodded, but clearly understood not a word. Mr. Saine wrote down Thomas. I took a breath, and before I let it out, had the whole thing. From Nguyen to Gwen to Win, easy as that. "Win. His full American name is Tom Win. W-I-N." I felt like an artist painting a brand-new picture.

"And a fine name it is, too," Mr. Saine said loudly to the kid, who was still staring blankly into our fog of too-fast words. *"Welcome to Pittsfield and Pittsfield Junior High School, Tom Win!"* His voice made the trophies on the shelf vibrate.

"Thank you." Tuan smiled politely. "Shut up," he said, a little louder.

Mr. Saine's jaw dropped open. So did mine. The room turned suddenly still, as if somebody had vacuumed out all the sound. My knees felt like rubber bands. Mr. Saine's face was gray.

Tuan kept smiling, though he did look uneasy.

"I . . . I . . . I . . ." I stuttered, my voice turned high like I'd just swallowed a balloonful of helium. "I think . . . I think . . . See, I told him, I taught him, that 'shut up' means 'be quiet.' I think"— I swallowed hard because my throat had become a desert — "he means you don't have to shout. A lot of people have been shouting at him, thinking it will help him understand. And it *doesn't* help, really. I taught him 'shut up' because it sounds a lot like Vietnamese bicycles." Mr. Saine's frown deepened. "He means to be polite. He learns fast. I even *told* him to say it loud, I—"

"All right, Harvey," Mr. Saine interrupted me,

76

still looking grim. His face was flushed. "I'll accept that." He said it, but I wasn't sure he meant it. "It's late," he said, using his normal voice. "Give these papers to your homeroom teacher, and, Harvey"— he took a deep breath—"*re*-explain 'shut up.' "

"Good night," the kid said, beaming.

We hurried out of the office toward homeroom, Tuan looking so cheerful I started to laugh out loud. He was positively the only kid in the whole school, in the whole world, maybe, who could get away with saying "shut up" to Mr. Saine. I was laughing, but my knees wobbled as I walked.

"Oh, by the way," I told Tuan as we reached the homeroom door, "your new American name is Tom." I stopped, opened my notebook, and wrote it down. "Tom," I repeated. "You."

"Tuan," he said. "Me."

"You have a new name, Tom Win. It's a terrific name. I made it up myself. I wish it was mine. I mean, like, it goes more with jeans and tennis shoes than the old one did. When you hit a homer at the bottom of the ninth with the bases loaded, they'll say, 'Win wins!' Tom Win," I repeated slowly. "The American you."

He stopped and thought about it. "Ba Noi say no. Father say no." The last bell rang.

"Do you want to be American or don't you?"

He nodded. "But Ba Noi say . . ."

"OK, then, just at school. Tom Win at school.

77

Tuan Nguyen in the privacy of your own home. Ba Noi won't have to know. To her and your dad you'll stay Tuan. No kidding, could I be Vietnamese and have a name like Harvey Trumble?"

He laughed and shook his head. "OK," he said. "Tom Win is me."

I rushed him into homeroom, a new kid.

The class, most all of them in their seats by now, looked up from what they were doing and stared at us.

"Uh, Miss Schwalbach," I said, handing her the papers Mr. Saine had given me, "this is the new Vietnamese boy we've been talking about, only he's changed his name. It's . . . uh . . . Tom Win. Mr. Saine says after homeroom he's supposed to go to the office for tests."

"Of course." She beamed at him. "So it's to be Tom Win?"

He glanced at me. "Yes," he told her. He held his hand out, and she shook it.

"We're glad you're here, Tom. People," she told the class, "I want you to be sure to welcome Tom Win cordially."

"That's not what I heard him called." Quint tilted back in his chair.

"Goes to show you don't know everything," I said very casual, like of course *I* did. "He's called Tom Win," I announced to the class. My kid, named by me.

Miss Schwalbach motioned to an empty place in the front row. "Sit here, Tom."

He sat. Tom Win sat. He could host a game show with a name like that.

While Miss Schwalbach read the Daily Bulletin, I could hear Quint telling kids around him to call the new guy Hot Dog, and he told everybody why. "They *eat* dogs where he comes from, you know. My uncle—who was there in the war—says so." The kids he told all gagged and yucked until Miss Schwalbach had to say, "People, act your age. Sometimes you sound like three-year-olds." Quint stuck his thumb in his mouth and started sucking it, and everybody around him laughed.

When the bell rang for first period, I delivered the kid to the office. Even though I said good-bye and wished him good luck, I was certain they'd be calling me out of science or language arts to help him with the tests. The morning went by without a messenger, though, and I guessed they'd given up on him or something. So I was really surprised when I got to the cafeteria at lunch and there he was, still smiling, sitting with Suzanna, eating a hamburger layered with pickles, mustard, and catsup.

"I just explained that hamburger isn't made out of ham." Suzanna popped a french fry in her mouth.

"It is cow," Tom told me. "It is good." He took another bite.

"Did the whole family change their names?" She

drew a smiley face in a pool of catsup with her last fry.

"Not yet." That might take some doing. We'd break it to them slowly. It was going to be some trick keeping the Tom/Tuans straight. The kid had this double identity like a spy. If only I could change my name, too. Tom Win would have suited me fine. "How'd it go?" I asked him. "Were the tests hard?"

He took a gulp of chocolate milk and blinked at the taste, licking his upper lip. "Words hard, Harvey. Numbers . . . weird."

That was a word I'd taught him by making faces. *Weird.* He liked it, but I guess it was like *shut up.* He didn't know what it meant. Numbers are a lot of things—like impossible. Weird, though, they're not.

But Mr. Tandy, our math teacher, sounded like he thought so, too. "A little strange," he said when class started. He smiled at Tom, who had finished his tests in time to come to the last class of the day. "Yes, class, you'd think that math was math the whole world over, but there are differences. I talked to our remarkable new student, Tom Win, this morning as he was taking some tests, and he suggested that some of our ways with numbers were unusual. I thought I'd check it out with the rest of you."

The kid looked at the floor, embarrassed.

"Tom, go to the chalk board. And Quint, you too, just to demonstrate the differences."

Quint, wearing his fabulous-me face, brought the kid with him to the board. They both took pieces of chalk and, when Mr. Tandy told them to, wrote down 675 divided by 15. Quint's problem looked normal: $15\sqrt{675}$. When he finished doing the problem, he looked over at the kid, who already had the answer. "Bizarre," he said. Mr. Tandy grinned. The kid had written, very neatly:

$$\begin{array}{c|c} 675 & 15 \\ 075 & 45 \end{array}$$

"Why'd he do it like that?" Quint asked, cocking his head. He shrugged. "I could have done it in my head."

"I expect he could have too, but that, of course, is not the point." Mr. Tandy was annoyed with him. "Now, both of you, write down twenty-five dollars."

Quint scribbled out $25.00 as fast as he could. Nobody was going to outrace him.

Carefully, the kid wrote: 25$00.

"More bizarre," Quint said, and everybody had to agree.

"You boys can sit down." I never saw Mr. Tandy quite so pleased. He grinned like everybody had gotten the extra-credit question right, or something equally miraculous. "And in Vietnam, when two thousand is written down it's . . ." Glancing first to the ceiling, where he always looks for approval, he wrote on the board 2.000. "There's a *point* after the thousand. On the other hand, they use a decimal *comma*. Thusly." He wrote 1,52. "Anybody think of a reason why one system is any better than the other, aside from the fact that you're used to it?"

Nobody raised a hand. He chuckled. "Neither can I. Isn't that fascinating!"

Quint rolled his eyes. "Knocks me out," he said sarcastically. A few kids giggled. Mr. Tandy laughed mildly, too. He knows not everybody is as crazy about math as he is. But he could afford to laugh. He was passing out a pop quiz. Aaarg.

"So, will this test count?" Caroline asked.

"Pieces of paper can't count. But I certainly hope you can. Any other questions?"

"Yes." Caroline sighed. "Do we have to take it?"

"You're wasting our time, Caroline."

All the time in the world wouldn't help. I knew I should have studied the night before instead of helping the kid learn English. We'd fooled around at Felix for a couple of hours, watched a little TV, sung with the commercials. I scratched on.

When Mr. Tandy said, "Exchange papers, please," a mass groan swelled out over the desks. I wasn't finished. A lot of kids weren't. The story problem was quicksand sucking me under.

Quint had already turned his paper over on his desk so no one could cheat from it. He was cleaning his fingernails with a toothpick.

Suzanna grabbed the kid's paper quick before I could. How she thought she was going to read it, I couldn't imagine. "What do I do about the commas and points?" she asked.

"If everything else is OK, grade them right. He'll get the knack of the mechanics soon enough."

"That's not fair," Quint complained.

Mr. Tandy started down the row, asking kids for answers and talking about problems.

"So, what do I do when Quint's decimal point's wrong?" Caroline asked. "Because one *is*."

"Mark it wrong. He knows better." Quint leaned over to look, not believing it.

When we got to the last problem, Suzanna raised her hand excited, and said, "Tuan . . . or Tom, whatever, got them all right. He did most of the marks our way. But he skipped the story problem."

"Terrific! Tom? The story problem?" Mr. Tandy pointed to it.

"I cannot read it."

Mr. Tandy looked at the ceiling again with a smile. He'd found another math person. Big deal. "I think it's *remarkable* that he's adjusted so quickly. Suzanna, mark the paper one hundred percent. And a big A. It ought to give him a real boost. He'll be able to read the story problems as well as you can before long."

"That isn't fair," I said. "If it's wrong, it's wrong. He's got to learn that." *I'd* gotten it wrong. And half the other problems too. There's such a thing as being too nice. I didn't want my kid spoiled. Besides, he'd kept me from studying. And he'd had all day Wednesday and Thursday to look at the books I'd brought him from school. He couldn't read most of the stuff, and so he'd probably spent all his time on the math I'd told him we were doing. He'd been *studying*. Hours probably. He didn't have anything else to do with me gone. "No fair," I said again.

Quint, who'd been looking pretty mad himself, suddenly crossed his arms and tilted his chair back. "Oh, forget it. He's no real hotshot," he said to me. "But he's no Zilch either." Then he looked at me funny. *"You* didn't teach him that stuff, did you?"

I smiled, genius in disguise.

"Your problem," Mr. Tandy said to the class, "is that you're not reading carefully enough. You're not following directions. I want you all to read that story problem over tonight and then to work it correctly."

Caroline opened her assignment notebook. It was plastered with puffy and smelly stickers. "Tonight's Friday," she said. "That's T.G.I.F."

"As good a night as any. Do this as part of your weekend homework. You *must* learn to follow directions." He chopped the air with his hand to pound out every single syllable. "Fol-low the di-rec-tions!"

Tom Win stood up at once. All heads turned to him. He turned his to me. What did he think he was doing? "Harvey?" he asked me.

I shrugged and stared down at the field of initials scratched on my desk. I didn't know what he was getting at. He was embarrassing me, standing there all by himself saying, "Harvey?"

"Where," he asked Mr. Tandy, "where is . . . Directions . . . so I can follow him?"

The bell rang, but even though it was Friday, the kids stayed in their seats and laughed out loud. He was a big joke to them. A hundred percent in math, and he thought it was time for Follow the Leader. And they weren't just laughing at *him*. I could feel it in the hairs on the back of my neck. They knew he was mine. They were laughing at me, too.

But when I looked up again, Quint had already gathered the kid up and was heading him out the door.

"Marbles," Tom Win called, holding up his bag of them. "Good night."

Quint waved. "This foreign person may be more interesting than I thought. I'll find out if my uncle is right. Anyway, your clone," he said, "has flown."

I couldn't possibly have followed them, even though *follow* seemed to be the word of the day. I'd have been late for work. But, I decided, the kid seems to be pretty smart. He'll figure Quint out in a hurry. It'll be good for him. I headed off, whistling, ready to push the pig's snout for luck before stacking boxes of vile green mouthwash high on the drugstore shelves.

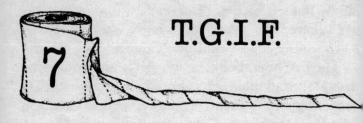

T.G.I.F.

Oooooooooouu, baby, baby,
Oooooooooouu, baby, baby,
You make me crazy.
Maybe, baby, maybe.
Oooooooooouu, baby, baby . . .

I couldn't actually hear Caroline sing. Maybe she
was just lip-synching to the record. She was dancing
like crazy, waving her arms like they were windshield wipers in a cloudburst.

With the tables and most of the chairs pushed

over against the walls, the cafeteria didn't look like itself. It didn't even smell like oranges and bananas. And half the big square ceiling lights were out—on purpose, I guessed, so the few girls who were dancing wouldn't look more than half dumb.

All the girls but Caroline had jeans on. She was wearing this red and black plaid dress and shoes with real heels on them. I mean, she looked different, so I couldn't help but notice. I watched her from the door for a while, wondering, off and on, how much time she'd put in on her math before coming to T.G.I.F. Probably as much as I had. I carry my math book home under my arm every weekend hoping I'll soak in the stuff without having to think about it. How much time Tom Win had spent, I didn't know.

He hadn't even come home for supper. While I was still at work, Quint had called. "He asked me to tell you," Mom said, "that Tuan is staying there for supper. His mother's in Springfield, but Wayne apparently wanted to talk to him about Vietnam. If I'd had enough chicken, I'd have asked them all to come here, but. . . . Then they're going to that party at school."

"They're going to T.G.I.F.?"

"Is that what it's called? He said if you came to bring marbles."

Bossy kid. I found the bag of marbles in the basement where I'd left it, but I'd had to work late, so even though I swallowed my pot pie and baked apple practically whole, it was all of seven-twenty before I got to school. The thing started at seven. Still, Quint and the kid weren't there. Or at least they weren't in the cafeteria. I tried the gym.

All the lights were on in the gym, at least, and nobody was going, "Ooooooooouu, baby, baby." So I walked in. The folding room-divider was pulled to separate the gym into halves. On one side kids were playing floor hockey, the red plastic sticks whaling on the yellow plastic sticks, with the puck skimming over the waxed floor almost as slick as on ice. A lot of action, but no Quint or Tom.

On the other side of the divider, kids—mostly boys—were lined up at the baskets, shooting. *POW-pow-POW-pow-POW*. It never stopped, a better beat than the music. Somebody heaved a ball across the room at the wall. It bounced down and off my head. I thought for sure *that* was Quint, but it wasn't—just an accident.

Wandering back into the hall, I pulled off my jacket and tossed it on top of the heaps of coats that lined the floor. Still, no Quint. What was he doing with my kid, anyway?

A high school guy was setting up a mike in the cafeteria, blowing into it and going, "One-two-three-testing." I went in to see what was happening and got myself in a long line for brownies and the cold, cloudy cider that Suzanna and some other girls were selling.

A few guys trailed in from the gym, thirsty, so, anyway, I wasn't the only boy around when the announcer finally got the mike going and boomed, "SNOW . . . BALL! OK, you guys, it's time for a huge, dynamic SNOWBALL!" He turned a record up so loud you could feel the beat as strong in your ankle bones as you could in your ears.

"OK, let's EVERYBODY form a big, round CIRCLE and ROLL IT!"

The girls kept talking to each other, chewing gum, glancing around as if they couldn't quite hear the guy on the mike, like if he'd speak up just a *little*, maybe. The boys poured cider down their throats and took their brownies in two bites, staring out at the empty dance floor like they heard the guy, all right, but could care less. Nobody wanted to be the first one out.

"Come *on*, you guys," the announcer pleaded. "They'll think I'm no good at this and *fire* me." I wondered how much they were paying him. He looked over toward the parent-types who were talking to each other at a table in the corner and not, at least, paying him a whole lot of attention. They didn't look ready to rise up and give him the hook.

"OK," he sighed. "OK. Listen, I know you guys

know how to do this. Just reach out and grab the hand of the kid next to you and before long, by some obscure law of physics, you'll have a circle and we can *spin*."

One girl tried to grab a guy's loose hand, and he leaped onto a chair and then to a tabletop, hopping across to another like they were stepping-stones. When he got to a table far enough away to be uncatchable, he began to dance all by himself, shuffling around, making crazy faces. Kids started to scream. I tossed my cider cup at the garbage can and crossed my arms.

A parent-type stood up. "Cut it out! If you can't behave, we'll close up right now," she said, her voice slicing through the music. "I've had just about enough of this nonsense. You settle down or that's *it*."

The kid ambled across the rest of the tables, jumped down, and fled to the gym. Out on the dance floor, though, a circle had started to form.

"ALL RIGHT!" the high school guy yelled. "Now all we need is one couple in the middle for us to snowball around." I was heading toward the door, sure I'd find Quint and Tuan—Tom—shooting baskets, when somebody grabbed my wrist and twirled me around and around the way we played Statues in second grade. It was Caroline.

Everybody was looking at us. I could feel them. I

mean, she was all dressed up, and I was me. My head spun even when we stopped.

"You scared to dance?" She smiled.

A kid next to me picked something off the floor and then whacked me one on my seat. "You chicken?" he asked, like the question was the answer.

"Looks like the yolks on you." The kid with him laughed.

"Me?" I laughed back, ha-ha. And to show them how scared I wasn't, I went with Caroline to stand in the center of the not-so-big snowball circle that was moving around and around. I picked my feet up and down while she cleaned unseen windshields with her arms. Over my shoulder I could hear girls giggling, so when the guy announced that the two kids in the middle should each choose somebody else to dance with, I escaped fast under a bridge of arms.

In the hall I stopped for a gulp of air. It felt like I hadn't had one for an hour. I was dripping sweat. The windows on the outside door were steamed up too. So I stood a minute, watching two kids writing on the fog with their fingers.

"Hey, Zilch!" I heard Quint call. "Didn't know *you* were changing your name, too. Very classy."

Behind me, next to the heaps of coats down the hall, he and five or six guys were sitting on the floor.

They were laughing at me like I was the Fourth Stooge.

"Say, S.E.," Quint said, "we watched you in there dancing with the girls. Our foreign friend here looked pretty shocked when he saw how Caroline swept you off your feet. I don't think that kind of thing's done in Vietnam."

I crossed my arms like I didn't know what he was talking about, but there wasn't much use denying it. "What's this S.E. stuff?" I asked.

Except for Tom, they all laughed again, louder. Like I wasn't just the Fourth Stooge, but the Fourth Stooge zapped with a chocolate cream pie.

"I've heard of egg on your face," Quint said without a smile, "but this is ridiculous."

"OK, what's going on?" I asked, as calm as I could.

"We shoot marbles, Zilch," Tom Win said, glancing at Quint to see if he'd gotten it right.

"Quint Calkins!" I yelled. I could have blasted him. He was grinning the way he'd done when he'd told the kid that a fork was a porcupine. Telling Tom to call me Zilch! "Listen, my name is . . ."

"Scrambled Eggs!" Suzanna came up behind me. "Harvey, why are you wearing a sign down there that says your name is Scrambled Eggs? I would have thought you'd choose something grander, like . . . Loverboy LaRue. I mean, what do you call someody for short whose name is Scrambled Eggs?"

That, of course, was when I realized it. The yolks
on me. First I stuck my hand into my back pocket.
The name tag from breakfast wasn't there. It must
have fallen out when Caroline was twirling me
around because it was just after that when the kid
slapped me on the seat of my pants. I reached back,
peeled it off, and crumpled it into a ball without
even reading what those girls had been reading as
I snowballed in the middle of the circle. I thought
about crawling under the stacks of coats and letting
them find me there hours later, dead of embarrass-
ment.

"What you guys doing?" Suzanna asked the kids
sitting on the floor.

"Ohhhhhh, Suzanna," Quint sang out, "won't
you shoot marbles with me?"

"Sure." She called over a couple of other girls,
and they all knelt on the floor next to him. "What
do we do?"

"You got some extras, Zilch?" he asked.

"Yes, sir. Yes, sir. One bag full." I was so glad to
talk about something else that I gave marbles to
anybody with a hand out. I sure didn't need them.
Nobody played marbles in Pittsfield. Nobody even
talked about them except fathers and uncles who
said how perfect it was in the old days without television when kids sat around shooting marbles in the

dirt. What a waste of time it was. We could have been at home with Felix, making some headway with the kid's grammar.

"I'll show you how," Quint told them. "This is a simple shooting game called Wall that we can do inside." Big authority on marbles. "Everybody puts one marble out here about a foot or so from the wall, and then we take turns shooting big ones *off* the wall, trying to hit one of the little marbles in the field." The little one Tom put out from his bag wasn't a marble at all, just a stone, a little rounded stone.

"I don't know how to shoot," one of the girls said, tossing a yellow and black one of mine at the wall, underhand.

"Show them, Tuan."

The kid opened up his palm and put the big blue marble on the tile floor. Then, resting just his thumb on the ground as a pivot, he flicked the marble with his middle finger. It ricocheted off the wall, hit one of my marbles, and flung it back into the pile of coats. Shooting with the cat's eye again, he picked off another and then another.

"In Galang camp we play a lot." The kid smiled proudly.

"My uncle used to play marbles," Quint told everybody. "He says he never saw anybody shoot that way. Everybody around here who plays at all shoots by putting their knuckles down flat on the ground and flicking the marble with their thumb. Like this." He flipped the yellow marble I'd given Tom, knocked it against a red one I'd given Suzanna, and put them both back in his pocket. "You always get the one you hit when you're playing for keeps."

"Let me try that," Suzanna said. "You got another marble for me, Harvey?" I handed her a green and white one.

It didn't seem like much fun to me, so I sat on the sofa of tossed jackets and watched. Quint kept calling the kid by his old name, Tuan, and telling everybody how bizarre his shooting style was.

I was leaning back, counting dots in the ceiling tiles, when Quint came over and sat down with me. He lowered his voice. "Listen, Scrambled Eggs, I got a little advice for you."

"My name isn't Scrambled Eggs, and I don't need any advice."

"A name's a name." He shrugged. "Whatever it is, you've got a problem."

"Caroline's no problem."

He grinned and started juggling three of my dad's old marbles. "Didn't say she was. Your problem is the kid." He pocketed the marbles.

"The kid? You're kidding. He knows more words every day."

"But he's not having any fun. You know? What's fun about being stuffed with verbs? I bet you even think he likes you."

"Likes me? Sure, I'm . . . his . . . "

" 'We all live in a yellow submarine . . .' " Quint began to sing loud.

" 'Yellow submarine,' " the kid sang on, laughing, " 'yellow submarine. . . .' "

"He learned that in Vietnam. Knows a lot of Beatles lyrics. I bet you didn't know that." I shrugged. "Listen, my advice to you is to give the kid a little fun. Let him know you're not just a word machine."

"I showed him my beer can collection. It's all in black plastic bags, so it doesn't look as great as when it's stacked, but I opened them up and showed him."

"I bet you told him all their names."

"Sure."

"What'd he say?" Quint's lip curled up in a half-smirk.

"He smiled."

"He smiles all the time."

"I know. That way you can't tell for sure what he likes."

"He likes *me*." Quint folded his arms and leaned back on the jackets.

"So?"

"So, I thought I'd help you have a little fun with him after T.G.I.F. I'd go, but my uncle's come to pick me up." He nodded toward the outside door. Wayne Calkins was leaning against it, flipping the ash off his cigarette. "He wants me to ride over with him to the Starlight Motel—find out why a guy who can't speak the language got hired when he didn't. Says he's going to tell them if it's Vietnamese they want, he can talk a few words of that, too."

Reaching behind us, Quint got his jacket, and from deep under the pile of coats, pulled out a large brown grocery bag. "So, this is for you," he said, like it was some big gift. "You'll have a terrific time with it. I gotta go now." He glanced over at his uncle, who was motioning for him to come. "Wayne'll be mad if I don't get out there soon."

"What's in it?"

"Toilet paper."

"Toilet paper! You've got to be kidding."

"What do you mean, kidding? Listen, two weeks ago—remember the night we won the game against Jacksonville twenty-one to twenty—well, I watched a gang of kids wrap a whole yardful of trees next door to me in toilet paper. The guy who lives there is captain of the football team. Anyway, they'd throw a roll up and it'd drape around the branches like silver icicles on a Christmas tree. I thought you could do Mr. Tandy's house tonight . . . or Caroline's."

"Caroline's?"

"Yeah, I'd like to come with you. She likes me.

97

But I gotta go. The paper's all yours." He got up. "And take my advice. Nobody's friends with a dictionary, even a dictionary named Scrambled Eggs."

Across the way all the kids were laughing, looking like they were having a terrific time bouncing little glass balls around. Quint called good-bye and ran toward the door just as Suzanna yelled, "I've *got* it. I think I've got it. I'm going to be a hotshot."

"Hotshot," Tom repeated, throwing his head back to laugh.

Wrapping trees in toilet paper. What a dumb idea. I'd seen TP'd trees, of course. Sometimes they looked pretty good, like they'd been hit by some kind of weird snow storm. But I wasn't about to TP Caroline's house. Especially if she liked me. Which, of course, she didn't. I picked up the sack and, wandering over to the door of the cafeteria, took aim and shot it at the trash can where the kids had been throwing their empty cups.

Swoosh. And the crowd cheered for Harvey Trumble, world-class athlete, as he shattered his career record and set a new one for the world. "Tell the vast television audience just what was going through your mind, Harv," the announcer asked, "when you sank that historic bucket?"

"Oooooooooooouu, baby, baby." The high school DJ must have had a very small record collection. Nobody was dancing.

The hall outside, though, was filling up with kids,

who were filtering in from the gym and cafeteria. They were either playing marbles or giving free advice. The game kept going, and Suzanna, Caroline, Tom, and I were among the last to leave at the nine-thirty closing. Suzanna had won three with the two I'd given her.

"Can I get more of these at the drugstore?" she asked me.

"Want a ride?" Caroline's mother was parked outside to take her, Suzanna, and a couple of other girls home.

We wouldn't have fit. Not without somebody sitting on laps. "No, thanks. We'll walk." As they drove off, I turned to Tom and said, automatically, "Car."

"I know." He nodded. "A Toyota."

I couldn't believe it. I hadn't told him that. I wasn't even a *good* dictionary. He was smiling, but I couldn't tell what kind of smile it was. Maybe he *didn't* like me. I couldn't ask him if he thought I was just a word machine.

"Wait here," I told him. "Don't go away." Dashing back just as the custodian turned the lock, I pounded on the front door. "I forgot something!" Mr. Bushel shook his head and turned away. "Please!"

Looking plenty disgusted, he frowned over his glasses and dug out a ring of keys to let me in. Then he watched as I threw open the door, hurried into the cafeteria, and produced my dazzling free-throw sack from the garbage.

"You got beer cans in there? Let me see." I'd had my picture in the paper once for my collection, and a lot of people know me for that. Some of them even think I drink the stuff, which is disgusting. But I sure wasn't going to let him look inside this bag, no matter what he thought. So, clutching it like a football, I hurled myself out the door. "Thanks!" I called as it clanged shut behind me.

"Let's walk home by the square," I said. "I want to show you the pig." It was only a block or two out of the way.

The night was dark. Only a small moon. And our street lights are changeovers from gas lamps, so they show you where the path is but don't make night seem like high noon, or even sunrise. The grocery bag didn't weigh much. Every few steps I'd fling it high so it would flip before I caught it. I was feeling great. This was better, much better, than acting out the meaning of *listen*, or even *sneeze*.

"And here it is!" I told him about the statue and how there are more pigs raised near here than anywhere else in the world. We ran up onto the courthouse lawn, away from the stores, to where Pitt Pig stood, barely reflecting the stoplight as it turned from green to caution.

A couple of cars drove by, but all the stores on the

square are closed by six, and so nobody was out buying dog food or bunion pads.

"Pitt Pig," I said, rubbing the creature's car-spring snout.

"Pitt Pig," Tom Win repeated. "Zilch. . . ."

"Tom, my name is not Zilch."

"Quint call you Zilch."

"Listen, Quint's just . . . " I reached into the bag, pulled out a roll of the toilet paper and heaved it into the air, expecting an explosion of streamers. It dropped down whole with a soft thud.

"What do you do?" Tom Win asked.

"This is called TP'ing." I loosened the paper from the roll so it would flow. "It's fun!" The paper was pink. I let it loose into the top branches of the oak tree next to the pig, and this time it caught before bouncing at my feet. "You want to try?"

He threw one that carried to the next tree over. "Why throw?"

"Because it's there." I wrapped the toilet paper around the pig's neck. It made him look like he'd just won the pink ribbon at the state fair. Rubbing the pig's nose with my sleeve, I told Tom, "I bet friend pig is bored silly standing here all year, cold and naked. I bet he'd like some more banners and festoons and song and dance. 'We all live . . . ' " Nobody was going to outdo *me* for fun. The pink roll arched up into the air again and emptied out midway down.

The second roll was blue.

"Duck!" A car rounded the courthouse square, so we pressed down behind the pig. It wasn't a squad car. Pittsfield has two. The lights moved past slowly, and since we were already crouched there, we tossed the toilet paper around the statue's little hog legs and wrapped its hams in blue.

All quiet again, we played high-flying pitch-and-catch, looping the rest around the branches. When that ran out, I grabbed the last roll, a green one. Carefully, I tore the paper loose, wound up, and tossed the stream of green toward the moon. IDENTIFIED FLYING OBJECT STREAKS INTO SPACE, the headlines read, LOCAL BOY SENDS PAPER PATH TO MARS, WHERE SQUAT RED PEOPLE SHRIEK WELCOME!

Suddenly we were in the spotlight. A real spotlight. It was bright and sharp and caught us like a net. The green roll fell, draping over the side of the pig and bumping down the courthouse lawn. Sirens whined in my ears, though I knew there were none in the air. It was dead quiet. My legs wouldn't move.

"What are you boys doing?" a voice called out. It might have been the light that spoke. That's all I could see. A car door slammed.

"Do we do wrong?" Tom grabbed my jacket. "Who is . . . ?"

Between us and the spotlight, a policeman

stepped onto the sidewalk. We couldn't see his face, just his shape, huge, motioning for us to come.

Tom said something to me in Vietnamese, the sounds catching in his throat.

"It's OK," I lied. "But we better go to him. He's a policeman."

"Policeman," Tom Win said.

When the policeman stepped out of the light, it still caught all the metal on him—his badge, the eagle on his cap, his gold-rimmed glasses, and the handle of the handgun slung on his hip. We walked toward him slowly.

"All right. What's going on over there?"

"Nothing," I said. I held my hands out to show they were empty.

He flashed his spot up at the trees. "Doesn't look like nothing to me." We looked at the paper loops connecting tree to pig to tree, and he was right. It didn't look like nothing. "What'll your parents say when I call them?"

I couldn't imagine what my parents would say. I didn't want to try. The sirens in my head moaned louder.

"My mother's probably asleep," I tried.

"I expect this'd wake her up." The policeman leaned back against the squad car and got out a notebook. "That must be . . ." He nodded to Tom.

"Right." I didn't know what name to give. "He's the kid from Vietnam, and he doesn't speak much

English yet. He didn't do anything. I mean, you know, they just escaped from . . . Please, don't tell. My dad would be mad."

"But what's the reason for all this?" Resting his hand on his holster, he nodded toward the pink, green, and blue.

"We were . . ." I began. I was going to say, "having fun instead of vocabulary," but then he'd have locked me up for bonkers. "We were . . . see, you know how they're always TP'ing football players' trees?"

He nodded.

"Well, I thought we'd kind of . . . decorate the . . . pigskin."

Either it was a twitch of the mouth or I saw him smile. "You ever do this before?"

"No, officer." I stood at attention. "And we won't again." I meant it, too. Tom stared at the policeman as if he was a ghost.

"All right. I tell you what you do." The policeman narrowed his eyes. "You clear up as much of this mess as you can, and hope for rain to wash the rest down from the branches. But . . . if I catch you again, it'll be a different story." He got back into the car and sat there for a minute looking at us before he turned on the ignition and drove away.

We didn't say anything. Just stood there, still scared, in the quiet square. I waited for him to round the corner again, this time on two wheels, blue lights flashing. The courthouse clock struck the first note of ten. And I began to pull paper. The fifth *bong* by, I realized he still hadn't come back with handcuffs and our parents. I kept pulling. But toilet paper is harder to take down than to put up. A lot harder. It tears on the dotted lines.

When the tenth *bong* had faded out all the way, I stopped pulling, one square of pink paper broken off in my hand. Turning to Tom, I said, "You know what? He didn't write our names down. He didn't take a phone number. And you know what that means?" Tom was leaning against one of the oak trees, his shoulders drooping. "It means he's not going to call home! We're free!"

The sirens in my head stopped completely and the bells started, high and happy. I looked at Tom and began to break up, hoping he would see how very, very funny the whole thing was. I felt as light as a hot-air balloon.

Scooping up as much paper as I could, I crammed it into the trash can on the corner and ran like wild, pulling Tom with me. Pittsfield has, after all, a second squad car.

We'd only gone a block, though, when Tom broke loose and dashed ahead fast. As I huffed along at a trot, calling after him, a car pulled up, driving slowly beside me. It was Quint and his uncle. Quint lowered his window. "Now, wasn't that fun, Zilch? Better even than TP'ing Caroline's house. But your guest has only been here a week. You really shouldn't get him arrested so soon. Naughty, naughty."

Wayne called out, "If the kid's old man doesn't do OK, I get his job." And they drove off, honking.

When I got home I looked in Tom's room to make sure he'd made it back. He lay curled up on the floor, eyes closed tight. Probably, though, he wasn't sleeping.

8 AND THAT, YOU GUYS, IS THE NEWS

AS WE WALKED TO SCHOOL on Monday, Tom was not smiling. Neither was I. "You laugh a big mouth at me," he said. "Quint say."

"Quint lied. I laughed because the policeman let us go. I was happy is all."

"Ba Noi say it bad. She say fingers one time dipped in ink not clean again."

"You mean you *told* her?"

He nodded. "I tell about policeman. She no understand why."

"What did you do?" Julia asked. "What police? What ink? I won't tell."

"Nothing. Nothing happened. Now, run ahead and play with your little friends." She stepped on my foot.

"We throw"— Tom didn't remember the words, but he tossed an imaginary roll of toilet paper in the air—"in tree and on . . . pork."

Julia's face lit up. Almost everybody had seen our streamers sometime over the weekend. "*You* did it? You're the ones who TP'd the *pig*?" And I could tell by the way she said it that we were going to be her Tell of today's Show and. She dashed off, arms wide, full of the story.

All weekend long Tom hadn't mentioned Friday night. Quint had talked to him on the phone Saturday morning. Then he'd gone off to their new house with his dad and grandmother and my mom to learn how to work their new washer and dryer and what the smoke alarm was like. The church was renting the place and fixing it up. The furnace was almost installed, so in a week they were moving from our place to theirs. They'd live in it free for six months and then start paying the rent themselves. That was the deal.

Mom showed Ba Noi what she could, but a Vietnamese man from Jacksonville, who'd been in the country more than a year, drove over to translate the hard stuff. I spent the day as a drugstore drone. Dad said he needed me more than they did.

Sunday the Quackenbushes invited the whole

109

Nguyen family over after church for dinner and a drive in the country to see the maple leaves. So, what with one thing or another, no time seemed right for talking about important things—like their new last name.

I wasn't sure what Tom was going to make of his first full day of school. I knew it was going to be different from the school he'd known before. My dad had asked about the one in Vietnam, and Tom had told him they always stood up when the teacher came into the room there, but then they sat at their desks memorizing facts and writing out problems and working on handwriting. It sounded like they mostly sat. Girls sat in the front rows, boys in the back. My dad thought it was terrific. I got tired just listening.

Anyway, I knew he hadn't had anything like our Social Studies class. Or Ms. Ward. She's young and pretty and always doing stuff to make us argue about what we're learning. "Try to see *both* sides," she says, "before you decide." The small wooden sign on her desk is painted, I SAID MAYBE, AND THAT'S FINAL.

"OK, folks, get out your reports," she said crisply when we'd settled down for our first class of the week. "The Monday Morning News Special is about to begin. Who's scheduled to anchor today?"

Two hands went up. "Splendid," she said. "Quiet on the set."

Every Monday morning we do a TV news program in Social Studies. Actually, it's just current events, but it's fun that way, and it keeps us pretty much up on the news.

"Thirty seconds!" Ms. Ward raised her hand, palm out. Charlie Gofen dashed up to her desk. His red and white T-shirt had a very long tie pinned to the neck, pulling it way down, very anchor-person.

"Fifteen seconds." Cammie Maclean joined him. They sat down and put on smiles. Ms. Ward pointed to them with a flick of the hand.

"This is Cammie Maclean . . ."

". . . and Charlie Gofen reporting from PJHS News."

"Our first live report is from . . ." Cammie surveyed the class. A lot of hands waved. "Caroline."

Caroline stood up. "A man flew a single-engine plane through the Arch of Triumph in Paris last week. He said he did it to complain about taxes. They arrested him."

I told about how the Pittsfield village board was going to vote on an ordinance to keep kids from skateboarding in the main business district, which would be a real bummer. There were a few reports on national and international disasters and near disasters.

"And now a special message from Ed Bood." Ed had been waving his hand like crazy. He stood up and shifted his paper from hand to hand. "Pittsfield residents were shocked Saturday morning when they saw that their world-famous statue, Pitt Pig, and the trees around it had been covered with . . . toilet paper." The class giggled, and everybody stared at Tom and me. Quint had been telling anybody who'd listen. I wondered if he'd called the police on us. "The TP'ing happened the night before the annual hog-calling contest at Chestnut Farms, which my Uncle Polk just happened to win by giving the biggest 'SUUUUUUUUUU-EEEEEEEEEEEEE!' that Pike County has ever heard." His uncle Polk couldn't have had much volume over Ed. That call would have knocked any real television station off the air and into Texas.

Ms. Ward cleared her throat and looked a warning at him.

"All Saturday morning," he went on, "rain congealed the yards—the *miles*—of pink, green, and blue streamers that covered the trees and world-famous pig, so that when it came time, newspaper reporters could not get a good clear shot of the renowned 'Pork Capital of the World' statue and the best hog caller in Pike County—as it turned out, my Uncle Polk, who had given the biggest . . ." He gathered up his breath.

"That's fine, Ed," Ms. Ward broke in. "Very interesting in-depth local report, but I'm afraid if you call again, the pigs would start answering, and we, frankly, don't have space in the room for both them and us."

Nodding, he went on. "No one knows if the hog-calling contest and the TP'ing were related because the culprits"— he turned to Tom and me—"were not apprehended."

Leaning over, I said, "See, it's OK, Tom. Everybody thinks it's funny." But he wouldn't look up. I put my arm on Caroline's desk behind me and, before I could pull it back, she'd written her name on my wrist in blue ink.

"Anybody have a commercial?" Cammie asked.

Rachael did. "Hi, I'm Rachael Warshaw talking to you about deep-down shine. Now, a polish made especially for braces. It's Moon Beam Brace Polish. Ummmmmm, what a great feeling, a bracing glow. It's Moon Beam from . . ."

"And next . . ." Charlie peered out over the raised hands. "Suzanna Brooks."

Suzanna stood up with her report. "Refugees are still leaving Vietnam." Kids shifted to glance at Tom, who was studying the top of his desk. It was hard to tell how much he understood. "A lot of people escaped when the United States left the war there in 1975. And they're still escaping. There isn't enough food, for one thing. And they're afraid of the Communists, whom they used to be fighting against. Some of them get shot when they try to leave in little boats. Or they get attacked by pirates on the South

China Sea." Tom rubbed his forehead with the tips of his fingers. "They were just people we heard about in the news until Tom came. Anyway"—she looked up— "we-are-glad-you-are-here." He understood that, for sure, and smiled back.

"Any other commercials?" Cammie asked. There was one. It was about an electric kite, just the thing for dull days when the wind isn't blowing. Four skill levels, from calm to tornado.

"And that, you guys, is the news," Charlie announced. We got out our books and moved on to Central America, its Crops and Conflicts.

All day Tom was quiet. I wondered if he really knew anything about pirates. Pirates were from old movies, the bad guys with eye patches, swords, and chests of gold. What would pirates want with my kid? All he had was marbles.

In gym he stuck mostly to Quint. When I tossed a ball to him, he bounced it off his head and passed it to somebody else with a kick from the side of his foot.

"Hey, Tom," the gym teacher yelled. "That's great. You'll have to help us with our soccer. It's a super game." The kid grinned. But it wasn't until math that he seemed easy again.

Mr. Tandy put him, Suzanna, and Quint in a group by themselves at the back of the room. He gave them books different from ours. "Let's see if we can get you three ready to jump ahead to freshman algebra next year. I think you're all up to it."

So, while the rest of us scratched and erased on our baby seventh-grade problems, those three sat back all smug, doing stuff the rest of us couldn't understand. Hot dogs.

After school, the kid disappeared upstairs with his math. He wouldn't even go to the basement with Felix and me. And since having fun hadn't worked out, I'd thought maybe we could do past tense.

At dinner that night, Dad said he'd pay Tom to work with me at the store. "Not many jobs out there for twelve-year-olds. Thursdays and Fridays after school. Most of the day Saturdays. You can show him the ropes, Harvey."

"Ropes?" Tom asked, leaning into the conversation, trying to understand.

Ropes, I thought. I don't know why you show people ropes instead of Blistex or boxes of baby aspirin. We didn't even stock ropes. A week ago words didn't seem at all bizarre, but even plain ones had started to have tilted meanings. By the time I'd thought what to answer, Tom was already translating a conversation between his dad and mine about how work was going at the Starlight.

The Vietnamese part sounded more like a song to me than talk. "Things fine, OK, good," the kid told my dad. Didn't sound like Wayne would be taking over right away, at least.

"And how were things with you today, Tuan?" Mom asked. "Did you like school?"

"The best," he told her, smiling politely. I'd heard Quint tell him after math, "Our group is best and I am best of the best." "No kidding," he added, and my mom smiled at me.

"You want to hear about *my* day?" Julia asked. "Has everybody forgotten me?" She took a gulp of milk that left a fat moustache.

"Oh, my dear, how could we possibly," Mom said, ruffling Julia's hair.

"All right, mite," Dad said as he pushed his plate away and gave her all his attention. "You just tell us what you learned today."

She glanced at Tom and me. "Nothing," she said, grinning wickedly.

"I pay good tax dollars for nothing," Dad fake-grumbled. "Shall I go to school and complain? You want me to raise Cain with Mrs. Broderick and her famous singing dog?"

"Well," Julia began fast, "if you *really* want to know. I learned that George Washington was the first president of the United States. I learned that he's on the dollar bill. I learned that he was the father of our country. I *also* learned something disgusting!"

I gave her the evil eye.

"I learned that Sandy Lazar has warts."

The kid was listening carefully. "Mr. Washington have many sons?" he asked.

Julia nibbled on her meat loaf and thought. "I don't know. Nobody said. He had false teeth and liked cornmeal mush cakes. Did he have kids, Harvey?"

"I don't think so. I know he didn't. No sons," I told Tom. "No daughters, either."

"How is he father?"

"I guess it's because he was there when the country was born. I'll show you his picture after supper. I'll show you pictures of *all* the presidents. You can learn their names."

"Father of Vietnam is a dragon," he explained.

"You're kidding." Quint had said they believed in dragons.

"A real one?" Julia speared her peas with her fork.

He nodded. "Father of Vietnam come from China many thousand years ago. He find green mountain, warm air. Banana, berry, rice. In forest is tiger, elephant, snake. In water is alligator. Place he find is Vietnam." He said something to his family in Vietnamese, and they both nodded. "Dragon like new land," he went on, "but he is alone."

"No lady dragon?" Julia asked.

"No. He find . . ." Tom closed his eyes, trying, I guess, to remember the words. He took a deep breath before saying, ". . . fairy princess. Mr. Larkin in Galang call her fairy princess. OK?"

"I guess."

"And did the fairy princess like the dragon?" Mom asked, clearing away the dishes.

"No kidding, she do."

"Did," I explained. "Past tense. *Did.*"

"She did. They marry. Have one hundred sons, brave like dragon, good to see like fairy princess."

"Now, that's a lot of sons," Mom said. "It would take a great deal of meat loaf and peas for a hundred part-dragon sons."

"Dragon leave princess," he went on.

"They got a divorce?" Julia frowned. "Fairy princesses don't do that."

"Dragon take fifty sons and go south to place of waters. Fairy princess take fifty sons and go north to place of mountains."

"*Then* everything was OK." Julia was waiting for the happily-ever-after.

"No. North fight south. South fight north." He pushed away from the table. "Still fight."

All that was over *there,* I thought. Not here. It was *then.* He should forget it. He doesn't need it, and I don't want to hear it.

But he kept going. "Many war. Many. Banana still grow. Tiger, elephant, snake, some still live in forest. Some forest die, some animal die, some people die. Many people in—" he took the sticker that said HELLO, MY NAME IS TABLECLOTH, and drew a stick man on it with bars in front of him.

Dad leaned over to look. "In jail," he said.

"In a dungeon," I told him. That sounded nicer.

"Four year my father in . . . dungeon," he said, taking my word. His father nibbled at a chocolate-chip cookie, not understanding. "He fight for south. Communists from north win war and keep him. Four year. He run away in suit of dead soldier. He make the soldier dead. Run at night. Sleep at day." The words were rolling out like he needed us to know. "He come home to Nha Trang. We hide him. We cannot stay in Nha Trang. Many people leave . . ." He took a breath as if he meant to go on, but he glanced at his father, and whatever he was going to say got stuck in his throat.

I stacked the dishes in the washer, put in the powder, and pushed the button, not knowing what to say. Maybe I should teach him future tense. Most of his past tense was war, running away, and sad. But it wasn't going to erase. He wasn't going to stop remembering. Some things you just can't forget.

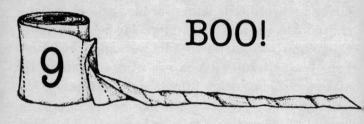

BOO!

"I'M TOOTHPASTE," Julia said. "Squeeze me." The funny thing is, she *was* toothpaste. At least she was dressed like a giant yellow tube of lemon-flavored PURE with a face hole cut in its cardboard cap. I'd pasted on a big red price sticker for $1.79. Halloween fell on a Saturday, and so, since school parties were Friday, Julia was in her first of two days as a tube of toothpaste.

"Oh, Harvey," she sighed, "you ought to be a beer can for Halloween like last year."

The genuine antique 1980 Pig Day T-shirt I was

wearing didn't count as a costume, even though I was sure it was pretty rare, probably worth hundreds of dollars to somebody. I bet they'd never even heard of one in Chicago.

"Seventh graders don't dress up," I told her. "That's for babies."

"Not even to trick-or-treat? You're short. You could get by with it if you had on a mask."

"I don't want to trick-or-treat," I lied. "Who needs to eat all that junk?"

"Mrs. Broderick is bringing apples to school. That's not junk. She's going to be Martha Washington with a cotton-ball wig."

Explaining Halloween to Tom wasn't going to be easy. I had to say something, though. It clearly wasn't normal heading off to school on a warmish fall day with a skipping tube of toothpaste. Especially when, right off, we ran into Frankenstein, a banana, and the Queen of Hearts walking with a gorilla in a tutu.

This was the last day I'd be walking to school with Tom. Monday he'd be on his own from his new house on the other side of school. Probably I wouldn't be seeing too much of him at all. I wasn't in his math group, and he liked that best. Maybe he wouldn't want to do any more drink-drank-drunk-but-not-think-thank-thunk stuff with me. Like Quint said, he probably didn't need me for a friend. When he moved out, it was like my part of the project was over and I'd earned a grade like C-minus. Or even zilch.

"Boo!" A skeleton jumped out in front of us, and I almost shed my skin. I just wasn't expecting it is all.

Tom looked stunned. "Why?" he asked me. Not a bad question.

"Well, on Halloween," I told him, "little kids wear funny costumes."

"Yes," he answered. It was the yes that means, "I have heard what you said." Nothing more.

"Halloween . . . is for scaring people," I went on, acting out scaring. Boo! like the skeleton. But Julia looked about as scary as a piece of toast. Halloween was harder to explain than *no kidding*.

"Yes?" He waited, I expect, for something more.

Across the street, two Draculas raced down the sidewalk, their capes flapping, their faces green. They shrieked. They were Billy and Simon without bicycles.

I couldn't for the life of me think *why* Halloween. Halloween just is. Every year it *is*.

"Tuan." Julia tugged at his arm. "*Look*, there's a fairy princess." She pointed to a little girl who was carefully stepping out of a car in front of the school. The girl waved a silver wand with a star, so that the ribbons sewn to it rippled. "She's a fairy princess— just like the one in your country who got divorced with all those babies." The girl had long blond hair that reached almost to the ruffle of her pink net ballet dress. On her head was a crown of silver sequins.

"Fairy princess?" he asked.

"Fairy princess," Julia said. "The wand gives it away."

This was not, I was pretty sure, how Tom had imagined his greatest-great-grandmother to look.

"Halloween," I explained.

All around us swarmed ghosts, bees, hobos, Siamese twins. I wondered if two weeks before, Tom could possibly have imagined that Illinois would be like this. A four-foot red crayon skipped by while the mother of his country waved her wand at a brand-new Chevy station wagon.

None of the kids at the junior high were dressed up, but Ms. Ward wore a witch's hat, had two teeth blacked out, and handed us each sacks of pumpkin seeds she'd roasted herself.

In art class we each got a small pumpkin to decorate. Manfred Chestnut's dad had sent in a pickup truck full of runts just for cutting into scraggle-toothed smiles. Tom's was different from everyone else's. He didn't know what a jack-o'-lantern was supposed to look like, and so he thought the long curved stem was its nose. Carving out tiny, tight eyes and feathery eyebrows close to the stem, he then cut in a long, sad mouth and a moustache with flipped-down ends. The art teacher held it up and said it was creative.

By one o'clock on Saturday, the real Halloween, Tom's creative pumpkin was sitting with the boxes and sacks of the Nguyens' stuff on our front porch, all set to move to the new house. Right next to the jack-o'-lantern was this fifty-pound bag of rice tied with a blue bow. We'd given it to the Nguyens for housewarming. One of those normal Uncle Ben's rice boxes would last them only about two days, and so they thought it was a great gift. Carrying it out slung on my back, I'd decided not to put Santa Claus high on my list of career goals.

I collapsed into the porch swing, pushed off, and cruised back for about five minutes, waiting for Jeff to drive up in the van so we could load up. Project Tuan/Tom was almost over.

Next to me lay the two old rubbery masks I'd brought down from Pete's closet. I mean, it *was* Halloween, kid stuff or not. I pulled on my favorite, a green-gray monster face with raw pink scars and gruesome fangs. I snarled to myself, and then, again, louder and meaner, as Julia flung open the porch door. She was still toothpaste, but now her tube was smeared with the Halloween candy that melts in your hands, not in your mouth.

"Is that you, Harvey?" she asked quietly.

"Narzak," I growled. "I am Narzak the Nasty!" Leaping out of the swing, I lifted her up and tossed her, screaming, into the air. "Happy birthday, earthling," I growled. Her party was set for two o'clock, and she was about to become the first earthling toothpaste tube in history to own a dog.

She didn't know it yet, but she'd begged so hard and so long and Mom and Dad had said, "Absolutely no. No, no, a thousand times *no*," so many times that they'd used up their supply. Mom's parrot tulips were just going to have to look out for themselves.

When Tom swung out the door with a Sears shopping bag in each hand, I tilted my monster face back and grinned out from under.

"Halloween today also?" he asked. I nodded and tossed him a big-eared sad-clown mask with a fat nose that honked when you squeezed it. He slipped it on.

We'd had to explain birthday parties to Tom, too. They don't have them in Vietnam, and he didn't even know when his birthday was. Julia sat on the edge of the swing. "People give you presents on your birthday."

"Julia!" I yelped.

"I didn't say *he* had to." Rocking the swing back and forth, she started to hum, "Happy birthday to you, happy birthday to . . ."

"Happy birthday, Julia Trumble, happy birthday to you." Quint dashed up the steps, a small suitcase in his hand. "Quint the Quintessential, here to startle, amuse, and confound your gullible guests!" He bowed. "Hi, Zilch. Surprised you're not dressed as Humpty Dumpty. How you doing, Tuan? You've changed, somehow. I can't put my finger on it." He squeezed the clown's rubber nose.

Jeff was late and Quint was early. I hadn't figured on his seeing me in my mask. Mom was paying him fifteen dollars to entertain the party with his magic, to keep the first graders from pouring lemonade into the house plants and pulling the stuffing out of the living room sofa.

Tom's father and grandmother came out the front door to wait for Jeff and their ride to their new home. Tom lifted his false face and spoke to them. They looked at him strangely and sat stiffly on the metal porch chairs. Ba Noi folded her hands in her lap.

"Oh, my, Julia, look, they're coming." Mom whipped out the front door, her cheek smudged with chocolate from the cake she was frosting.

A Raggedy Ann skipped up the front walk, orange yarn wig flapping, a red triangle painted on her nose, a birthday box under her arm. "Play outside in the leaves for a while, will you, dears," Mom said, with a smile. "Quint, I'm delighted you're early. Harvey, I didn't recognize you. You must get something from the drugstore for that complexion. Perhaps your father has some Green-Off in stock." Then she honked Tom's red nose, waved at the

126

Nguyens, and disappeared into the crepe-paper streamers. Quint followed her.

By the time Julia had torn the wrapping off a jumprope with felt carrot handles, Quint was back on the porch. Around his shoulders he'd tied a black cape lined in satiny red. From his empty hand he produced a small bouquet of paper flowers and gave them to Raggedy Ann. She hid her face in her hands and giggled.

Ba Noi smiled, and then laughed, when she looked out to see a washing machine skipping up the sidewalk carrying a box tied with a silver bow. Sandy Lazar had his head and arms sticking through holes in a carton he'd painted white with black knobs. An old diaper hung out of a circle cut in front to swing open like a door.

"Sloosh!" he yelled at us, waving his arms. "Sloosh, sloosh!"

Quint dashed into the house again, but by the time Sandy had reached the porch, Quint was back to greet him. Opening the washer's door, Quint stuck his arm in and pulled out red, yellow, green, purple, and polka-dotted scarves, one after the other after the other.

"Hey," Sandy yelped. "Where'd those come from?" He almost fell on his face trying to bend over and look inside. But he was boxed in. While the kid-flow stopped for a while, Quint's magic didn't.

He threw a plain old rope into the air, and it came down with a knot in the middle. Tom and I tugged our masks off to see better. It was good to smell air again that wasn't rubbery, and to feel that you weren't hiding inside somebody else's face.

A skeleton charged up the steps.

"Hi, Ina," Julia told it. "My mother is paying Quint to make us laugh."

Quint tickled one of the skeleton's broad white ribs, and the skeleton laughed. He was earning his money.

"Teach me magic?" Tom asked him.

"Sure. Just sit Zilch up there on the porch railing, wave a wand, give him a push, and he'll disappear." He laughed like that was supposed to be a big joke.

All of the kids had arrived, and so Julia started ripping off the rest of the wrapping paper. She got a mechanical camel, a set of paints, a book, and a loaf of plastic French bread that laughed when you picked it up. Quint headed to the other end of the porch to set up his magic table.

I grabbed the neck of his cape and pulled him over to the corner.

"Listen, I don't know why you're doing it, but would you stop trying to keep the kid from being my friend."

"He doesn't need a friend. He's got math." He smoothed the wrinkles out of his cape. "Besides, my uncle Wayne's right, you know. They don't belong here."

"I guess you're mad that he's better in math than you." Quint couldn't keep up with him. Couldn't begin to. Mr. Tandy let us go at our own speed, and Tom's was so fast it was like he had jets on his ankles.

"No way. He just studies more. I could do it easy if I tried."

The little kids were getting restless, tearing paper, taping ribbons on each other's noses. The skeleton was starting to cry.

"One thing," he went on, "they're going to leave this town. They aren't Win, they're Nguyen, and they can't pretend different. The grandmother," he nodded toward her, "can't talk to anybody. The father hardly says anything. The kid is going to math himself into orbit way above *you.* Then they'll leave. You'll see. My uncle'll get that job, and—"

"Quint!" Julia called. "Aren't you going to put on a show?"

"And you'll be best in Mr. Tandy's class again. Gifted. Big deal."

Tom was standing behind his father, just waiting for the van to come and take them away, not a part of the party anymore.

"Harvey, it's time!" Mom said from the kitchen. "Come help." So I hurried in to get the big present, glad after all that Jeff was late. This I wanted to see.

129

Mom handed me the cardboard carton with Julia's new singing sensation in it, and I headed back to the porch, carrying the box high above my ears so the kids couldn't see inside. I set it on Quint's magic table like she told me.

He was blowing and twisting balloon animals, handing out yellow poodles and orange swans. When the sleeping-dog box was settled, though, he held his arms out wide and announced, "Here now is the grand astonishment of the day. Small wonders, cross your legs and sit tight!" The washing machine squatted, unable to sit. Julia rolled her tube up to her waist to free her knees. "Ladies and gen-

tlemen!" He bowed deeply. "I, Quint the Quintessential, magician extraordinaire, will now attempt to produce from simple, everyday balloons, one Genuine Carnivorous Canine!"

The cross-legged kids in front of him blinked and gasped. Taking a small pink balloon from a sack, he puffed it full. Over and over he made the same shape, twisting them together to make a whole batch of what really did look like a string of hot dogs from the butcher's. "And what, my clever friends, are these?"

"HOT DOGS!" they yelled, pleased they could tell.

"Absolutely correct. Now, I have on this table, one box, completely and totally empty." He pointed to it with a wand.

"Show us inside," the skeleton called. But Quint went on. "*Completely* and totally empty. *But*, when I drop in this string of magic see-through hot dogs ..." He tossed them lightly into the box. "... and you say the magic word—frankfurter—those hot dogs will, in one magic instant, turn into ... but, let's hear that word!" He whipped the kids into action with his arms.

"FRANKFURTER!" they yelled.

"I can't hear you." Quint cupped his ear, trying to catch the word.

"F R A N K F U R T E R !" they yelled again, stretching their heads far forward to make it louder.

The box made a strange, sniffly sound.

Quint nodded to Mom. And they must have worked it out ahead of time because, as he waved a wand, she reached in and lifted out the carnivorous canine puppy. Brown and fuzzy, with a white spot under his chin, he was so new you couldn't tell what kind he was. He yelped, though, and it was clear the fur wasn't stuffed with foam.

"Happy birthday from Dad, Harvey, and me," Mom told Julia, who shrieked and struggled to her feet so she could clutch him.

"His name," Quint announced grandly, "is Frank."

"Frank Furter?" she asked, suspiciously.

"One and the same."

"It is not. His name is Fluffy." She gave the dog a pythonlike squeeze.

"If you hug him too tight his tail will come off," I warned her. "And Fluffy is a dumb name for a dog."

She put the puppy on the floor, holding the kids back with her arms and one outstretched leg.

"Here, Frank," Quint called. The dog wagged its tail, which didn't even look loose.

"Here, Fluffy," Julia called, and the puppy waddled toward her, pausing only to lower its fluffy bottom to wet the floor.

"Ready to go?" Jeff Zito bounded up the front walk. "Sorry to be late. I had a long wedding reception. Beautiful ceremony, though." He stopped at the top of the porch steps and looked around him. An orange swan popped. Julia picked up Fluffy for him to see. "And I've come in the middle of yet another celebration. Happy birthday, Sunshine," he told Julia, patting her on the cap.

The Nguyens stood and greeted him. Figuring this was it, I picked up the rice to save it from carnivorous canine attack. When I lifted it, rice poured out of a hole that hadn't been there when I'd set it down. I covered the flow fast so nobody would notice.

"Anything wrong?" Quint asked with an innocent smile.

I shook my head. That hole hadn't been made by magic.

Tom gathered up a couple of shopping bags, ready to start off for the van, but he stopped and put them down. Reaching into his jacket pocket, he took out his sack of marbles, poked in it for a minute, and pulled out the big blue cat's eye.

"Happy birthday, Julia," he said. "Happy birthday to you."

THE SNOW DRAGON

10

I DON'T KNOW why they didn't let him go with them. I mean, she's his mother, after all. I would have bugged everybody until they took me along. What's one day of school? If you've got a sore throat, they keep you home and don't think a day's such a big deal. But when Tom's father told him to do something, he did it. I never heard him try to argue out.

They'd been in their new house three weeks, and Tom's mother and the baby were finally flying into Chicago on that same early Saturday morning plane. Jeff had decided to drive them to Chicago this time on the day before the flight so the Nguyens

135

could go shopping for groceries. They'd stay overnight with friends of his. There were a lot of things Ba Noi missed eating that she couldn't get at Quackenbush's grocery store. She longed for them even though she knew, Tom said, that "the tree is now a boat. It cannot be a tree again." This meant, I think, that she understood things, even food, wouldn't ever be the same as in Vietnam. Still, she really wanted to eat some squid again—or octopus, I couldn't quite tell which.

That's because Tom had drawn pictures, and we'd looked in dictionaries and a batch of cookbooks in the library. Finally we'd come up with a list of groceries to give Mr. Quackenbush. Most he didn't have, didn't even know where to order.

So, squid (or octopus), bamboo shoots, lemon grass, and rice paper were all on the list they took. And so was a kind of fermented fish sauce Tom called *nuoc man. That* Ba Noi wanted more than anything. They were going to buy bottles and bottles of it at a Vietnamese grocery store in Chicago.

On Friday, Nam Nguyen got a day off from work, Ba Noi bundled up to go traveling and grocery shopping and talking to people who could understand her words, and Tom came to our house to spend the night.

For two days it had been snowing, the first snowfall of the year, coming down slow but steady. Tom liked to look at it, but he wasn't used to its cold. He'd never felt snow before, only seen pictures of it.

After we'd worked straightening the stockroom, I got him to go down to the basement to play a few games with Felix. No verbs, though. No kidding.

The snow fell like crazy—fat, wet flakes that settled in clumps. Julia and her friends were out rolling around in it as Tom and I headed downstairs. We started off with one of Pete's Zagnab programs. I was just about to locate the treasure, too, when I typed in that I wanted to turn (L) instead of (R) and Felix said, SORRY ABOUT THAT, HARVEY, YOU HAVE JUST FALLEN PLOTCH INTO A PIT OF TEN-HEADED, YELLOW-LIPPED, DIRTY-TOENAILED, SLIME-GREEN SERPENTS. YOU ARE DEAD, DEAD, DEAD—ALMOST. And when I couldn't find the steps back up the pit's scummy sides, Felix called me a DROOLING, DITHERING DOLT. Then he let me know I'd been serpent-swallowed and said, OK, HARVEY, CARE TO PULL YOURSELF TOGETHER AND TRY AGAIN?

. I told him no, thank you, and showed Tom how to program Snow Falling on Pittsfield. What you do is you print PITTSFIELD in the middle of the screen and then make little random *'s appear until *ping-ping-ping,* Pittsfield has a white-out.

"It seemed like," I said, not knowing at all if I should say it, "it seemed like when your father left, he was kind of, I don't know, like, mad at you." It was nosy of me, but if I was going to be his friend, I had to try to help.

Tom started fiddling with his bangs, which were getting too long. "Yes, I . . . Every day, I am telling him what to do, how to get to place, what sign say. In Vietnam, son not tell father what to do. At the store he cannot read names on cans. I must tell him."

TYPE IN YOUR NAME, the computer flashed.

TOM WIN, he wrote. Then he spaced twice and typed, TUAN.

" 'This telling is wrong,' my father say. 'I am father. You are son,' he say. He thinks my mother will not like it. He thinks it will be bad for baby." He pushed the OFF button. Felix sighed and turned gray.

"Look, he'll learn pretty soon."

"For him English is hard. I *must* tell him. That is why I study. To help. Mr. Larkin in Galang say that is the way. My father and Ba Noi say I am *too* much American. I must be American. I must not be American. I do not know what to do."

"I know he'll get used to it. Jeff's working with him. They'll all learn to speak English. And your mother will like it."

He shook his head. "Father say he, Ba Noi, and my mother more happy with more Vietnamese. I think they want to go to Chicago. Many Vietnamese there."

"To stay?"

He nodded.

"They won't do that. I know it." I didn't know it, though. What if that's why they'd gone to Chicago early, to look for another place to live? Jeff had been talking about something to my mom and dad, I knew that much. And Quint was always saying they'd go.

"I . . ." Tom wrinkled his forehead and looked glum.

"I am worried?" I guessed.

"Yes. I am worried."

"Worry won't help." At least if he was worried they would leave, that meant he wanted to stay. "You want to go to T.G.I.F. tonight?" I didn't know if that would cheer him much. He'd only been that one time, the night of the TP. "They'll be shooting marbles on the flat mat." Caroline had even added MARBLES to the poster because so many kids had started playing.

"No. I study."

"You *always* study." He did, too. It must have taken him days to learn all those Central American cities. It did me. "OK, if you don't want to go. But let's go outside for a while, at least." I felt like moving. "You ever build a snowman?" I knew he hadn't.

"No." He laughed. "Before I come here I think snow fall in big pieces from the sky." He threw his arms out wide. "*That* big! I not know about the . . ." He turned Felix on, pressed ENTER a couple of times, and then brought up a string of *'s.

"Flakes, snowflakes."

"Yes."

"Come on. Grab your coat and gloves. We'll gather us enough snowflakes to build a man."

Tom pulled on his big green coat, a knit cap, and a pair of gloves. I wore Pete's warm old down jacket with the patches.

The snow hadn't stopped. It was almost dark, but you could still see it falling by the street light. Julia and her friends, Sandy and Ina, had started to build a snowman. When they couldn't roll the first ball any farther, though, they'd just left it and started pushing drifts together to make a fort.

"What'd you think?" Julia called when she saw us. We stepped back and looked. What they'd made was this wavy wall about two feet high and fifteen feet long. Fluffy ran along beside it, barking a tune I couldn't recognize. Julia would have known if I'd asked her.

"Looks terrific," I told her. "Looks like some kind of fortress for extremely short people, cat-sized."

"It is dragon's tail," Tom said.

Julia frowned and walked the length of it. "Where's its head?"

He pointed to the ball they'd rolled halfway across the yard. "He lose it—there."

So, while Julia and her gang of three kicked their wall around to make it even wavier and patted the top into a kind of scaly point, Tom and I waded through the snow to roll the ball into position. It was right under the street light. Packing, poking, and patting on more and more wet snow, we built a dragon neck thick enough to hold his round ball head. Tom gave him ears and a wide flaring snout. He looked ferocious.

"I'll get some more stuff," Julia said. "He needs more. Wait."

People driving by waved and honked. I mean, you don't see too many snow dragons swimming under Pittsfield street lights. We were beginning to look like snow creatures ourselves when Julia finally came out with a mammoth carrot and a long purple scarf.

"It's his cigar," she said, poking the carrot into the dragon's mouth. "So he can breathe fire." Then she wrapped the purple scarf around his neck. "So he won't catch cold."

Next she pulled off her mitten and shook out of it into her hand the blue cat's-eye marble. "And here's his eye. He's a one-eyed dragon. He sees all." Setting the blue wedge just right, she stuck the round eye in the middle of the dragon's icy forehead.

I shivered. It was, of course, a magic marble that would turn the creature live and snarling, whip loose his massive tail, and start him puffing clouds of silver steam through his fat orange cigar. DRAGON ROAMS PITTSFIELD ALLEYS. FEAR STALKS CITIZENS.

Julia plopped onto his back, grabbed the ends of his scarf, and yelled, "Giddy-up!" Fluffy snapped at the fringe. But the dragon just sat there coldly and stared.

"It's getting late, my dears," Mom called from the front porch. "How about tomato soup and grilled-cheese sandwiches? You must be frozen blue."

"We've just made a red-hot dragon," I yelled.

"Listen," I told Tom, "we'd better take the marble in." I reached for it.

He stopped my hand. "No. Julia put it there. It is her marble. The eye look at snow first time. Look all night. Tomorrow mother come."

After supper and homework in front of the fireplace like two Abraham Lincolns, we climbed the steps to the second floor. I had studied math on a Friday night. I couldn't believe it.

Mom thought Tom'd go upstairs to the room where he'd first lived, but I wanted a sleepover so we could talk. Tom's bag of things was on the bed next to the window. And he was taking out the Cubs'

pajamas I'd given him as I carried in the little TV and put it on the table between our beds.

Nothing much was on, though, so after about a half-hour of flipping channels, I turned out the light. Crawling under our heaps of covers, we listened to the wind blow through the empty maple branches.

"I like beds. I never knew beds before here," Tom said. We could hear the sleety snow scrape at the window. Our fiery dragon had probably swum through ten-foot drifts, slithering over vast obstacles—curbs, fireplugs, parked squad cars—to talk to Pitt Pig, whose feet were stuck in concrete.

"Tomorrow you'll all be together again. Everything will be terrific. Your little sister will probably say her first words in English, did you ever think about that?"

I waited for him to answer, wondering if maybe I'd talked too fast. But that wasn't it. By his deep, heavy breaths I knew he was asleep. The house was quiet except for Tom's breathing and the furnace in the basement huffing away. It's funny having somebody else in your room when you're not used to it. You know they're there even when it's dark.

Pretty soon I knew it even more. Out of the quiet I heard a soft, high moan and then this choky, panting sob.

"Tom," I called softly. I didn't want to scare him, but I didn't want him to keep crying, either.

"Tom, it's OK. You're here. Nobody's after you."
I used to be afraid at night that a crow was dive-bombing me, and so I know how he felt. I think I know how he felt.

Tom turned over in bed, threw back the covers, and drew himself into a ball. His Cubs' pajamas were all twisted.

"Tom." I flicked on the light between the beds.

In the middle of a sob he opened his eyes. He frowned for a minute, blinked, and then almost smiled as he leaned on his elbow. "I wake you," he said. "I am sorry. It is . . ." He pressed his fists on his eyes and lay his head back on the pillow. "I think I am not here. The sea is so big and I am there. I am on the boat and they shoot. If they catch people being escape, they kill them. My uncle Truc . . . they . . ." He pounded his hand on his chest. "We left him in the waves. Ba Noi cry all, all night. All day. I cry, too."

I turned off the light, not wanting to look at him sad, and remembered how Quint had said the Nguyens were cowards because they wouldn't go down the escalator. I asked him, "Were there pirates?"

"I do not know . . . pirates. Men jump in boat. Take all. Hurt . . ."

"That's OK. You don't have to tell me. I just wondered about the pirates."

"Snow on your window sounds like scratch of rats. At night rats look for rice on boat." He stopped talking, and I thought he had gone back to sleep. "I smell the seasick. I am afraid we fall in the waves." The wind began to sound like rats to me, too, sharp-toothed and hungry. "I am sorry," he said, "I wake you."

When I was little and would wake up soaked after the crow attacks, my mother would change my bed and tell me to think good thoughts. And I would think hard about pink cotton candy and the time I won a stuffed penguin that leaked a trail of little white chips all the way home from the carnival. And I'd think about hitting a home run with three kids on base or about swimming underwater the whole width of the pool. But I wasn't sure what would be good things to Tom. If he thought about the happy stuff in between war times, that would only make him sad because he couldn't go back. Maybe ever. Besides, one thought would lead to the next and the first thing you know he'd be on that little boat again with the rats.

"Are you OK?" I asked.

"I am OK, no kidding," he told me. Those were my words he was saying, but they meant different things to him. I knew that.

"Good night, Tom. Tomorrow's going to be terrific."

"Harvey?"

"Yes."

"You are not Zilch?"

"Right. Zilch is *not* who I am. My name is also not Scrambled Eggs."

"Harvey?"

"Yes."

"I am not Tom. I decide. I will be American. I will. But my name is Tuan Nguyen."

Not my kid at all. "Yeah," I said, "I guess I knew."

11 PHO TAI AND PUMPKIN PIE

AFTER A NIGHT of snow, our creature looked more like a stretch-tailed ghost than a dragon. His spine was rounded, and he seemed to cruise half underwater. Even though it was Saturday and usually a work day, Tuan Nguyen and I both stayed home for the big welcome. In the blue sky and warming day, we'd swept the steps, front and back, cleared the walk, and even shoveled the snow off the driveway before Julia came outside with Frank F. Fluffy.

The puppy plowed through the snow, nose tilted down, disappearing into the deep, except for his brown swishing tail. Yipping a kind of shorthand

"Jingle Bells," he was clearly tone deaf but showed a lot of promise with the volume. His real talent had turned out to be his teeth, with which he'd gnawed off both of Zachary's wings. Julia didn't seem to mind, though. Poor Zach had become a flightless has-been.

Waving the carrot that had dropped into the snow, Julia announced, "Our dragon gave up smoking last night. He spit his cigar out." I shook the snow dust from his purple scarf, and Tuan woke him up, blowing the white off his eye.

A snowball zipped past my ear. Nobody was in sight in the direction it came from. No whole body, anyway. Down the block, Quint's blue coat stuck out from both sides of a tree that was skinnier than he was.

"Hey, your disappearing act needs work!" I yelled, and he fell, arms straight out, like a chopped-down tree, into a drift.

We ran over to check him out, and when we looked straight down on him, he opened his eyes and said to Tom—Tuan, "How come Mr. Tandy's newest math sensation isn't inside studying?"

"Because I just got up," I answered. "Besides, I never study. I am gift-ed."

"Very funny," he said, but he laughed anyway. He got up and shook the snow off. "Thought you might like to know my uncle got a job yesterday. In Jacksonville. He got it from a want ad, and he's gonna move there, get an apartment. He says there are more jobs in Jacksonville." Quint smiled his smirk. "And more Vietnamese, too, for those who'd like to move to a place where they talk Vietnamese."

"Cut it out," I told him. "Be nice, for just once. Tuan's mother and baby sister are coming this morning."

"I knew *Tom*'s mother was coming. Who's this Tuan person?"

A horn honked down the block, and Tuan searched the street for the blue van.

"He's going back to using his old name. He'd never even told his family about being Tom."

Tuan nodded and stepped out into the street to look again.

It was empty of blue vans. And nobody else was expected. We weren't having a big party the day Tuan's mother and sister came. Instead, we were going to let them get to sleep early. People would say hello to them at the big Thanksgiving festival we have every year at the church. That was five days away. Every year Miles' Bakery roasts all the turkeys, and families bring other food from home.

"Are we too late?" Caroline and Suzanna slid down the street, one carrying a yellow rubber duck and the other a small brown bear with a plaid bow. Caroline had her hair all tucked under a fuzzy white cap that looked as soft as new kitten fur.

"We'll baby-sit. Babies are crazy about us."

Caroline squeezed the duck and it went, "Meow."

"Not yet," I told them. "It's just noon. Probably it'll be an hour or so."

"We could always build a snowman," Caroline suggested, pulling the furry cap down over her ears.

"Or a fairy princess to go with the dragon," Julia said. "I'll go get a wand."

"Bizarre." Quint looked after her.

The warm air made the snow damp and heavy, good packing, and so we started rolling balls to build with. A fairy princess, or whatever.

"Cut it *out*, Quint," Suzanna yelled.

"I'm going to blast you!" Caroline told him. He was tossing handfuls of snow down the necks of their coats whenever their backs were turned. The two of them started pelting him with snowballs.

"Come on, you guys, we won't get anything built that way."

"But, Zilch, this is fun."

"Sometimes you've got really weird ideas of fun, you know that?"

He plucked the marble eye from the dragon.

"Hey, put that back. It's mine." Julia marched toward us with a construction-paper star on a stick. She'd taken it down from her bulletin board.

Quint dropped the big blue marble like it was scorching his fingers. But then he scooped a handful of snow around it. "Just a touch of magic, my small friend." He patted her on the head. "A little frozen prestidigitation."

I mean, how could she argue with *that*? He was putting on another show.

After packing one, he made two more and threw the first in the air, the one with the marble. I think. Then he threw another. Then the third, juggling them higher and higher, no sweat.

"Question is," he went on, keeping the balls moving, "which one has the dragon's all-seeing eye inside? Who can say?"

He caught them and held them out for our inspection. "Ladies and gentlemen, is it snowball number *one*?" He pitched it up, caught it behind his back, and then flung it against the base of the street lamp. When the snow crushed and fell away to the sidewalk, there was a marble there—but it was red.

We all gasped.

"What, red? Did it change colors? Or is it, then, in snowball number *two*, round and cold and icy?"

First he tossed it high. Then, catching it in his fingertips, he wound up like a pitcher throwing your basic fast ball, and hurled it at the dragon. Its soggy snout collapsed neatly into the sea. "Whoops! As you can plainly see, it's not in ball number two." So far as we could see, nothing was in ball number two. I gathered up the snow from the snout and threw it, grapefruit-sized, back at him. It caught him on the shoulder, but he brushed the slush off and grinned.

"Unless there has been some major mistake . . ." He packed his last snowball tighter. ". . . it must be hidden in number . . ." And before we knew it, the snowball was coming. Somebody should recruit Quint for the majors, no kidding. He's got an arm. "Catch it, Zilch!" he yelled, and it came at me straight as radar.

I ducked and the ball skimmed past. It whizzed between Tuan and me into the street like a missile, just as a car came driving by. It wasn't the blue van we'd been waiting for, but it wasn't just any old car, either. It was one of Pittsfield's two squad cars. *The* one. And the officer inside was the same guy Tuan and I had met before in the night under the stars, moon, and toilet paper.

Quint's snowball slapped into that squad car's windshield with a crack that sounded like a branch snapping in a storm.

The policeman hit the brakes, skidded in the slush, and swerved totally around into the curb.

If I could have, I would have melted and run down the gutter.

The policeman didn't have a spotlight this time. He didn't need it. Even getting out of the car, his eyes held us. Everyone but Julia, who ran for the house, dog at heels, yelling, "Quint killed a car!"

"You two again?" The policeman shook his head at Tuan and me. "On to bigger things?"

153

"They didn't throw it," Caroline told him.

"They just didn't catch it," Suzanna said. "*He* threw it." We all turned and looked at Quint, who wasn't smirking. He looked scared.

"I didn't throw it at you." Quint stuck his hands in his pockets like he'd never had them out. "It was an accident. Your car ran into my snowball."

"No kidding," Tuan said.

The policeman took off his hat and rubbed his forehead. "What you're saying is that it's *my* fault? I don't believe this." He shook his head. "You might have caused an accident," he told us. "You know that, don't you?"

We didn't have time to answer.

Tuan started talking suddenly, excitedly, in Vietnamese that sounded like one long singing word. And he ran. The blue van was turning the corner, its horn honking.

"That's his *mother*," I told the policeman, who did not look impressed.

"*And* his baby sister," Caroline went on.

"They've come all the way from Vietnam, and he hasn't seen them in months. This is their first *day* in this country," Suzanna told him. "You wouldn't spoil that because of a snowball, would you?"

The policeman sighed. "I can't believe I'd give you two another chance."

Mom hurried out the front door and started down the steps, hesitating as though she didn't know whether to save us from prison or welcome the Nguyens. She chose the Nguyens.

"Thank you, officer," Caroline said. "You are a good person."

Tuan's dad got out of the van. Then his grandmother, and, finally, a small, pretty woman carrying a baby.

"Can I go now? I'll probably never see you again for the rest of my life," I told the policeman.

"You," he pointed at Quint. "You keep those snow bullets off the street." He tipped his cap at Tuan and his family, who stood in the driveway looking at us with interest. Then he pulled his car off the curb and drove away.

Caroline, Suzanna, Quint, and I ran over to meet Tuan's mother. But as we hurried up, another woman climbed out of the van, carrying yet another baby. Then two more men, and after that, a kid about ten or twelve years old. He was carrying a guitar.

I didn't know where they had come from or where they were going. Tuan was racing around, talking to them all.

Jeff hopped out of the driver's seat. "Come meet the Nguyens," he called to us.

And that's what he'd been talking to Mom and Dad about. The people were from Galang camp, and they were staying at our house until our church found a home for them.

Quint wasn't the only one who'd noticed. Jeff had seen that Tuan's dad and grandmother were lonely, too, and had been trying for weeks to get another family to join them. It hadn't been all that easy, and he didn't want to announce that they were coming if it turned out they weren't. The two men were cousins of Tuan's dad, and all of them were Nguyens.

We said hellos, but nobody shook hands. We were going by the old rules.

Suzanna and Caroline gave the duck to one baby, the brown bear to the other, and then hurried off, waving. The babies stared back silently as they were hurried into the warm house.

Propping his guitar against the van, the new kid began whooping and scooping snow up and flinging it in the air so it covered his hair like a white cap. Quint hurried over and showed him how to pack a proper snowball. He did his three-ball juggling act, lobbing each one over the van.

"Come on, Quint," I told him, "you know you're teaching him trouble."

Quint watched the new boy shiver as he pushed a fat, funny-shaped ball together with bare hands and heaved it just past the van's rear tire. "Listen, Zilch, he can't be an Illinois kid and not know snowballs."

"His name is Minh," Tuan explained. "He speaks almost no English . . . now." Picking up the guitar and talking to Minh in Vietnamese, Tuan headed him toward the house, taking charge.

"They *will* stay, you know," I told Quint, feeling suddenly smug and happy. "They'll *all* stay. Maybe Minh'll show you how to play the guitar . . . or how to do your extra-credit math."

He tried to stuff a fistful of snow down my back. "Zilch, you . . ." But I whirled around and got a handful of my own.

"The name," I said, shoving my clump of snow under his collar, "is *Harvey*. I've had all the Zilch and Scrambled Eggs I ever want to hear."

He yelped and shook the snow out. Then he reached in his pocket. I didn't know what he was going to try next, but I balanced on my toes, ready to skid him down the sidewalk if I had to. With sleight-of-hand magic, he slipped something into my pocket. "Give that thing to Julia, will you?"

I drew it out carefully. It wasn't a soft-boiled egg, a water balloon, or even a blob of just-chewed gum, but the old blue marble, not chipped to bits in the street at all.

"Didn't it smash the police car?"

"Nope. Kept its eye shut tight in my pocket all the time. It would have made cobwebs of his windshield, for sure, and we'd all be down in the pokey right now. See you around." He ran, and called back over his shoulder, "S.E."

I showered him with snow.

Because she had known there might be a batch of people, Mom had fixed her huge pot full of stewed chicken, an enormous bowl of rice, and two apple-sauce cakes. There wasn't room enough for all of us in the dining room, so just the adults ate there, and the babies. Tuan, Julia, Minh, and I sat at the kitchen table.

As Tuan showed Minh how to use a fork, Minh asked him something.

"The name is porcupine." Tuan grinned at me.

"Fork," I told Minh. "Fork." I scooped food into my mouth and held out the fork again, repeating it.

"Fork," Minh said, smiling. I wondered, just for a minute, if he might like to start a beer can collection better than anyone else's in town. Even mine. And if he might be good at learning *I* before *E* except after *C.*

"Can he come to the Thanksgiving dinner?" Julia asked. "Mom is taking three pumpkin pies."

"Pumpkin? Like my . . . ?" Tuan drew a long-stem nose from his face like the one on the jack-o'-lantern he'd carved.

"Right. It is made from that, only without the moustache." I wasn't sure what he thought he'd be eating on Thanksgiving. Fried funny faces, maybe.

"My father and Ba Noi bring back many things to eat. I think we bring *pho tai* to the dinner."

"Pho tai?" Minh recognized a familiar word among all the strange ones. He was struggling to keep the rice on his fork.

"What's *pho tai?*" Julia asked him.

158

"Soup," Tuan told her, "made with cow."

"Beef."

"Made with beef, rice noodles, a little lime."

"*Pho tai*," Julia repeated. "They didn't have that at the first Thanksgiving."

"When is first?"

I'd forgotten he didn't know. We'd studied all that in fifth grade, but not again in seventh. "On the first Thanksgiving Day the pilgrims ate with the Indians," I told him. "The Indians had lived in this country for a long, long time. The pilgrims were new here. They came from England."

"Far away," Julia told him.

"We came from far away," Tuan said.

Minh's head was drooping. He looked very sleepy. I was not going to give him my hair dryer if he took a shower.

"At the first Thanksgiving," Julia explained, "the Indians brought five deer. The pilgrims cooked turkeys, corn bread, and eel pie. I learned that yesterday."

"*Pho tai* OK?" Tuan asked.

"Sounds good to me. *Pho tai* and pumpkin pie." I leaned back, full. "Hey, Tuan, after Minh goes to sleep, let's you and me go out and build a snow pig."

Tuan grinned. "OK," he said. "No kidding."

About the Author

JAMIE GILSON, the popular author of numerous Archway Paperbacks including *Harvey, the Beer Can King; Can't Catch Me, I'm the Gingerbread Man; Do Bananas Chew Gum?* (winner of the 1982 Carl Sandburg Award and the Charlie May Simon Children's Book Award in Arkansas); *Thirteen Ways to Sink a Sub* (A.L.A. *Booklist* Reviewer's Choice); and *4 B Goes Wild,* has a firmly established reputation in the world of children's books as an entertaining and contemporary novelist.

A native of Beardstown, Illinois, Ms. Gilson grew up in small towns in Missouri and Illinois. Following graduation from Northwestern University, she taught junior high school and wrote for Chicago radio stations. Currently, Ms. Gilson lives with her husband, Jerry, and three children in Wilmette, Illinois, where she writes for *Chicago* magazine, lectures and holds writing and poetry workshops in the Chicago area.